THE ICY STRAIT

THE ICY STRAIT

AN ALASKAN NOVEL

NEAL DASTRUP

RMR PUBLISHING HOUSE
Provo, UT . Las Vegas, NV . Excursion Inlet, AK

THE ICY STRAIGHT
AN ALASKAN NOVEL

Copyright © 2014 by Neal Dastrup

Published by RMR Publishing House
1061 East Provo Canyon Road
Provo, UT 84604
nealdastrup@yahoo.com

ISBN 978-0-9857740-1-1

First Edition Published 2014

Typeset by *www.wordzworth.com*

Printed by Worzalla Printers
3535 Jefferson Street
Stevens Point, Wisconsin 54481

DISCLAIMER

The Icy Strait is a work of fiction and should not be construed as representing real persons, places or events. Some names of real persons and real places appear, but only for the purpose of creating a setting to tie in with historical circumstances. None of the real people or real places were actually involved in the fictional portrayals found in the book. All of the events described were created from the author's imagination.

CONTENTS

FOREWORD

Alaska. The Great Land. America's last frontier presents the ultimate backwoods lure for many men who seek manly adventures. In the spirit of Jack London, we are magnetically drawn to *The Call of the Wild.*

This is a book of Alaskan adventure and intrigue. Fiction? Maybe. Tall tales? Perhaps. Unsuspecting sport fishermen clashing with a troupe of scheming Alaskans? For sure. Read the book and follow up by scheduling a trip to the *Alaskan Bear Lodge.* You might be surprised as to what is real and what is not.

For many years, my wife and I have lived on a ranch on the banks of the Provo River, just a few miles downstream from the *Sundance* mountain resort. It would be difficult to find a more beautiful place on planet Earth, yet I constantly find my mind and heart drifting back to Alaska.

Utah's Provo River is one of just a few blue ribbon fisheries in the United States. Originating high in the Uintah Mountains at remote Washington Lake, the river winds seventy miles through pristine, snowcapped mountains until reaching its final destination - Utah Lake. Teaming with Brown and Rainbow trout, why would any angler search for greener pastures? My book explains why.

Consider for a moment that a healthy Utah trout weighs two or three pounds. Compare that to an Alaskan Chinnook salmon, which sometimes exceeds thirty pounds. Further, contemplate that Alaska's bottom feeding Halibut can tilt the scales from a hundred up to as much as four hundred pounds.

The fish breeds in Alaska vary from Lingcod to Rockfish and from Dolly Varden to Steelhead trout. The mind numbing list of fish types and sea life creatures in our forty ninth state goes on ad infinitum.

While the size and weight of Alaskan fish get more than their share of attention from sportsmen the world over, a more significant draw (to me, at least) is the untamed nature and variety of adventures that await travelers venturing to the far north. Unknown excitement and sometimes danger lurks around every bend in the river, across every body of open water and around every Sitka spruce in the old growth forests.

Every bit as exciting as the rugged landscape is the ever changing cast of characters living in the villages and hamlets in my favorite recreation destination on earth. For a multitude of reasons, my preferred port of call has long been Alaska's Icy Strait.

ACKNOWLEDGMENTS

There would be no *Icy Strait* without salty characters and I have borrowed liberally from my experiences with Alaskan friends as well as some from the lower forty-eight. Gary Liddiard and Frank "Randazzle" Hulme are my tried and true fishing buddies and long-time companions. Grantley Moore captains *The Equinox* out of Juneau; Jared Long owns and operates the *Salmon Run* in Excursion Inlet; Ponch Marchbanks lives and works in Gustavus; Keith Skaflestad and his family operate T.E.C.K.K. Outfitters in Hoonah; and Wes and Sue Tyler own and operate Icy Straits Lumber in Hoonah.

Many others mentioned in the book are also Alaskan characters who give me pause and make me long for the Great Land when I am away. John Crabill, the inventor of *Johnny's Seasoning* and proprietor of *Johnny's Dock* (my all-time favorite sea food restaurant) is my Excursion Inlet neighbor and Bruce Gordon and Monte Mitchell live a ways further up the inlet.

Dusty, Devin, Tyler, Jeremy and Shawn are my sons and sons-in-law and, in addition to being great fishing companions, they help with some of the work around our *Alaskan Bear Lodge*.

I am grateful to Lauren Parker and Scott Cameron for reading, editing and commenting on my manuscript as it was written, giving ideas and constructive criticism to help me through the process.

I am also indebted to Leslie Nelson who, after reading *My Implausible Memoirs*, suggested I write another book using her favorite Wallace Erwin poem as inspiration. Mr. Wallace's poem, *A Nautical Extravagance*, appears on the following pages for your reading enjoyment and to give you an idea of the perils we "manly men of the sea" face on a daily basis.

DEDICATION

Although she does not appear as a character in this novel, my wife Brenda has been my constant anchor and sail since 1974 and she has always allowed me the freedom and encouragement to enjoy a life of fun and adventure. This book is dedicated to her.

—NEAL DASTRUP, AUTHOR

A NAUTICAL EXTRAVAGANCE

By Wallace Irwin

I stood one day by the breezy bay
a-watching the ships go by,
When a tired tar said, with a shake of his head:
"I wisht I could tell a lie!

"I've seen some sights as would jigger yer lights,
And they've jiggered me own, in sooth,
But I ain't wuth a darn at spinnin' a yarn
what wanders away from the truth.

"We were out in the gig, the Rigagajig,
jest a mile and a half to sea,
When Cap'ting Snook, with a troubled look,
he came and he says to me:–

"O Bos'n Smith, make haste forthwith
and hemstich the fo'ard sail;
Accordeon pleat the dory sheet,
For there's going to be a gale.'
"I straightway did as the cap'ting bid –

No sooner the job was through
When the north wind, whoof
bounced over the roof,
and murderin' lights, she blew!

"She blew the tars right off the spars,
And the spars right off the mast,
Sails and pails and anchors and nails
flew by on the wings o' the blast.

"The galley shook as she blew our cook
straight out o' the porthole glim,
While pots and pans, kettles and cans
went clatterin' after him.

"She blew the fire from our gallant stove
and the coal from our gallant bin,
She whistled apace past the cap'ting's face
and blew the beard off his chin!

"'O wizzel me dead!' the cap'ting said
(And the words blew out of his mouth);
'We're lost, I fear, if the wind don't veer
and blow awhile from the south.'

"And wizzel me dead, no sooner he'd said
them words that blew from his mouth,
Than the wind switched round with a hurricane sound
and blew straight in from the south.

"We opened our eyes with a wild surprise,
and never a word to say –
In changin' her tack the wind blew back
the things that she'd blew away!

"She blew the tars back onto the spars,
and the spars back onto the mast;
Back flew the pails, the sails, and the nails,
which into the ship stuck fast.

"And 'fore we could look she blew back the cook
straight into the galley coop;
Back dropped the pans, kettles and cans,
without even spillin' the soup.

"She blew the fire back into the stove
where it burnt in its proper place –
And all of us cheered as she blew the beard
back on the cap'ting's face.

"There's mor o' me tale," said the sailor hale,
"As would jigger yer lights, in sooth,
But I ain't wuth a darn at spinnin' a yarn
what wanders away from the truth."

CHAPTER ONE

THE FISHERMEN

Recruiting deck hands, fishermen and sailors from Russia's Kamchatka Peninsula port was not a passive task for Captain Samuel McGee. It was an adventure in intrigue. Since purchasing an old relic of a ship an ocean away from the Gulf of Alaska, he was desperate to find a few hearty and hale men with enough talent and stamina to operate it on the open sea. Getting home to the Icy Strait to restore it was proving to be a bigger challenge than he thought.

The long, lean, unshaven and unkempt Australian born immigrant scoured the alleys along the ancient cannery docks that dotted the shores of the Sea of Okhotsk. He was searching for the men who, just hours before, had pocketed his enlistment bonus after signing a contract of employment. The captain was ready and anxious to leave port, but his crew was nowhere in sight.

During the search, he thought about replacing what now appeared to be a gang of undisciplined hired hands, but time was running short. From experience, he sensed that it would be a more difficult undertaking than to simply retain those he had already employed. He deduced that his deteriorated tug would have to be manned with a band of vodka drugged misfits.

It had been only a few days since he had enlisted his small troupe of rag-tag youth, most of whom he had found huddled together for warmth in the squalor of the busy Russian seaport. Even though they initially appeared to be an economic way for the captain to man his ship, the project was becoming more expensive than what he bargained for. Under the unforgiving pressure of time, he finally paid a ransom to local authorities to help him round up the miscreants and get them onboard his ship.

McGee's persona was that of a harsh master, but his recruits did not fear living the infamously harsh lives of galley slaves once they were on the high seas. Even though they might have been intimidated by his unique style, their greatest foreboding was the angst of having to subsist for long stretches at a time without their beloved alcohol. They were set on having one last binge before leaving port.

It was past midnight when McGee and his hired authorities finally located the recruits. As had been expected, they were drunk and passed out behind one of the seaside bars. The Kamchatka Border Guard considered the inebriated men's signed contracts and cashed enlistment bonuses to be sufficient conscription. Their conclusion was helped, of course, because McGee had the presence of mind to pay them partially in advance and the balance upon delivery. The captain secretly hoped this initial experience with his motley crew was not a harbinger of things to come once they were out on the high seas.

When they were a safe distance from port, McGee resorted to using fear to sober up his crew.

"Throw all excess baggage overboard!" the captain bellowed to his First Mate, above the roar of the stormy sea. Then, spitting in the face of the nearest cowering deck hand, he followed up with "...an' 'ow much d' ye weigh, mate?" To a man, they soon became submissive and followed their captain's orders.

Months at sea exposed sailors to Mother Nature's most extreme elements and many a seaman could only survive by finding humor in such an otherwise terror filled life. Whenever a good jingle was discovered, the crew committed it to memory and they alternately recited verses to one another.

From one such narrative that was titled *A Nautical Extravagance*, Captain McGee adopted his seafaring nickname of Cap'ting Snook and from the same poem, he rechristened his newly purchased vessel, the *Rigagajig*.

For self-aggrandizement, he frequently commanded his misfits to recite his adopted poem and they reluctantly did so, as if it were a mode of conciliation to their volatile captain.

Once the swabbies procured their sea legs, Cap'ting Snook made haste through the Bering Sea past the Pribilof Islands. He then passed through the Aleutians between Akutan and Unimak Islands; then across an unseasonably rough sea in the Gulf of Alaska. Finally he and his crew found refuge in the calmer waters of Alaska's Inside Passage, where he discretely anchored close to his fishing business in Elfin Cove.

■ ■ ■

Meanwhile, down in the lower forty eight, events were transpiring that would eventually introduce an unrelated group of sport fishermen to Snook and his summer drama:

THE ANGLER

Standing waist deep in the Provo River in mid-June, his fly rod bent to the maximum, Gary Liddiard was about to land an oversized rainbow trout

As he reeled down his line and then pulled the rod skyward, a loud and energetic band of river runners riding the rapids in old patchwork inner tubes rushed around the bend, blind siding and knocking him off balance in the swift river current. The boisterous band continued downstream, all the while cursing the fisherman for being in "their river" and, thereby, causing them to briefly veer off their watery course.

Liddiard was livid. His detractors were vocal. As had happened time and time again, the river proved to be too small for both river rafters and fishermen to peacefully coexist.

To no avail, the drenched angler unsuccessfully grasped for his prize fly rod, but it had washed downstream behind the inner tubers. What should have been a peaceful and fulfilling commune with nature had become a frustrating and expensive morning for Gary. Something had to change! The fisherman vowed to find a better location to enjoy the peace and solitude he felt he deserved in his retirement years. Juvenile inner tubers be damned! Liddiard was not about to let them determine the quality of his fishing obsession. He alone would make that determination.

Within hours, he contacted and scheduled a trip to a highly recommended fishing lodge on the banks of Alaska's Inside Passage. He would be there in the middle of the Coho run in late July.

THE ACTORS

Tempers shortened and horns intermittently blared as congestion in the notorious L.A. morning traffic increased to epidemic proportions. With no chance of escape, Dusty O'Neal and Tyrone "T-Bone" Jameson patiently sat in their car, as if they were trapped in a huge parking lot. They grew increasingly restless and felt anxious when, along with hundreds of others, they were penned in without a chance to escape the Ventura Freeway. They had hoped to get to the movie studio in time for make-up. However, as time slipped by, they knew their hope was in vain.

It was the final day for shooting their new film, a remake of *Wyatt Earp*, and this was not the best time for them to show up late. Notwithstanding, getting there on time now appeared to be out of their hands. They would never be able to get to the studio through such a motionless gridlock. Today, the producers, directors and the other actors and supporting staff would have to wait for the stars to arrive.

Construction was the culprit causing the delay and the over-heated road crew seemed oblivious to the needs of the motorists. Since the flag men controlling the flow of traffic knew that they would not be getting out of the hot sun any time soon, "why," they sadistically reasoned to one another, "should anyone else be allowed to vacate this misery any faster than us? Fair is fair! Right?" Staring down the motorists became their form of enter-tainment and their method to retain their sanity.

Finally, in accordion fashion (or more descriptively, in imita-tion of an oversized motorcade slinky), the rows of steaming, overheated vehicles started moving. Within a few yards, however, everyone again came to an abrupt stop. Everyone that is, with the exception of the car directly behind the famous actors.

The cigar smoking, bigger than life character sitting behind the wheel of his beat up '84 Oldsmobile was in deep and animated conversation on his cell phone. Distracted, he slammed loudly into the rear of the actor's car. The metal-to-metal crash caused the emergency bags on Dusty's late model BMW to deploy, attesting to the degree of impact of the two vehicles.

After freeing themselves from the pressure of the ballooned safety bags and regaining composure, Dusty mumbled to Tyrone, "Do you remember our fishing trip to Alaska a few years ago?"

"Yeah, I remember," replied Ty. "That was a better time than this!"

"It was a week in Paradise," continued Dusty. "I've had it with this L.A. traffic and smog... and this damned, non-stop mass of humanity."

"Let's make a phone call then," T-Bone grinned. "That dude at the lodge might still have a room available, even at this late date. His number is in my cell phone directory... I'll make the call right now."

"Good idea, Ty. I'll call the studio and have them contact Incident Management so we can get this mess cleaned up. We've put in some long days and it's time we took a break! We've earned it."

THE HUSTLER

As it always was in the Arizona summertime, the mid-afternoon hot spell was consuming. The desert climate was especially disagreeable for one California Bay Area transplant who always found the heat suffocating, unforgiving and without justification. He could find no vindication for not being able to comfortably breathe.

Dr. Franklin Hulme, D.D.S., was aptly nicknamed Randazzle* by one of his old college buddies. Masculinely attractive by all measures, he was athletic and well-conditioned. Even in his sixties, he retained a full head of dark, often mussed hair. The D.D.S. was intelligent and knowledgeable by any standard, and he was wealthy. In short, the handsome, mustachioed dentist considered himself to be a "hustler," even for a man his age.

"I'm roasting in this heat," the perspiring dentist stated to his wife. "Even laying around the pool doesn't help. I've got to get out of here and go back up to Alaska, just to cool off!"

"That's your excuse every summer," laughed his beautiful wife, Gloria. She knew that when her husband's mind started longing for a fishing trip, there was nothing she could say or do to change it. He had been making annual excursions for over a decade to different fishing camps along the Inside Passage and she knew this year would be no different.

6

"I personally love the Arizona heat," she continued. "I really don't understand why anyone would choose to leave the comfort of an air conditioned home for a primitive place like Alaska!"

"Yeah. It's primitive all right. Long, cool days. Sun drizzled rain. Bears, eagles and whales. World class boating and fishing... you're right. It's hard to understand."

The conversation unceremoniously ended when Randazzle dove into the cool water of the swimming pool. Even with a few unseasonable storm clouds rising in the western sky, the sweltering heat outside the family pool remained stifling.

The next morning, Randazzle got up early. "If I'm not in Alaska," he thought, "I can at least enjoy a weekend fishing at the lake." Careful to not wake his wife, he dressed quietly and went into the kitchen to make a sack lunch. When finished, he grabbed his dog by the collar and slipped silently into the garage.

The handsome dentist carefully hooked his fourteen foot aluminum boat, the *Sea Nymph,* to his Range Rover and proceeded to back out into what had become a torrential desert downpour, with winds that were blowing upwards of fifty miles per hour. Discouraged, Randazzle reconsidered his solo fishing trip and pulled his vehicle and boat back into the garage. He turned on the radio looking for a weather report and listened as the broadcaster said the storm would go from bad to worse during the weekend. He slumped behind the wheel in his car for over half an hour before wisely deciding to scrap his weekend fishing adventure.

After much contemplation, Randazzle went back inside his house, quietly undressed and slipped into bed. Cuddling up to his wife's back, now with a somewhat different adventure in mind, he softly whispered "the weather out there is terrible!"

"Yeah," Gloria sleepily replied without turning over. "Can you believe my idiot husband is out there fishing in that?"

At that moment, Randazzle decided it was past time to pack his bags and return to Alaska! He also knew it was time to re-think his life.

*Randazzle–Noun: Derived from combining the adjective 'randy' and the verb 'dazzle.' Randy–Adjective: Lecherous, displaying excessive interest in sex. Dazzle–Verb: amaze, astonish, bedazzle.

CHAPTER TWO

RANDAZZLE

Hoping to recharge his diminished confidence by engaging in a romantic interlude along his way to Alaska, Randazzle took a commercial flight from Phoenix to Seattle. He then took a taxi from the airport to Bellingham and, upon arrival, entered the ferry terminal. Once inside, he made preparations to board the Alaska Ferry *Columbia*.

Hulme's travel agent booked his departure two days prior to the time the other *Alaskan Bear Lodge* fishermen chose to depart by airplane. This allowed him time to enjoy a cruise up the Inside Passage and still reach Juneau the same day as the others in his group.

Hoping for additional adventure, he opted to travel by way of a different route. He envisioned himself starring in a plot of conquest. One that resulted in an exciting tale he could share with the new friends he would make at the lodge. The aging dentist was desperate to reestablish himself as a "player."

Randazzle knew he looked good. He always looked good. Nevertheless, as was his habit, he double checked himself from every angle in the ferry terminal men's room mirror. First, he checked his teeth. Then he checked his hair. To be certain of himself, he rechecked his smile. Finally, growing in self-assurance, he engaged in mirroring a collage of facial expressions and then stepped back to review his profile. He was set.

Satisfied that he was at his best, the lifelong tomcat instinctively sprayed three shots of breath refresher into his mouth and then revitalized his already overpowering *Elsha 1776* musk cologne. After leaving the men's room and boarding the *Columbia*, the D.D.S. was on the prowl for young feminine talent.

At 6:00 p.m., the four hundred eighteen foot ferry disengaged and left port, right on schedule. The huge marine vessel was beautifully outfitted and very similar to a small cruise ship in appearance as well as its state-of-the-art accommodations. Alaskan citizens take pride in their intracoastal public transport system and Randazzle was pleasantly surprised with the impressive quality of the ferry.

His stem to stern reconnaissance ended on the seventh level deck at the rear of the ship where he spotted small groups of coeds setting up camping tents in the open air section. They were busy affixing their tent stakes to the boat's metal surface with layer after layer of duct tape. Even though the ship had over one hundred cabins available for rent, most of the young travelers chose to pitch camping tents in lieu of paying the extra few dollars to rent a berth.

"The mating game has become so easy," he smiled to himself. "These days, it's like the chicks hang out a neon 'available' sign. It's not like it was back in my college days. Now, it's more like picking low hanging fruit. Easy."

The common areas inside the *Columbia* were more than adequate for Randazzle's romantic aspirations. In addition to two restaurants (one a short order snack bar and the other an upscale dining room with panoramic views), the facilities included a theater, a gift shop, and a beautifully outfitted piano bar. Toward the bow, there was a common area with reclining overstuffed chairs that were lined up in rows to allow scenic views for the passengers.

The ship's cabins ranged from small efficiency bunk bed apartments to larger and more elegant staterooms. Boasting a twenty million dollar construction cost in 1974, the Lockheed built vessel propelled through the Inside Passage at a comfortable eighteen knots-per-hour. As mentioned, Randazzle was pleasantly surprised.

When the ferry reached port in Wrangell, the wealthy dentist spied what he had been looking for. From his binocular view on the seventh deck balcony, he watched a pair of Scandinavian twin sisters board the *Columbia*. Going over his mental check-list of feminine attributes, Randazzle deemed them both perfect. Visually, they were worthy of his attention from top to bottom.

Since he exuded the confidence of an affluent professional, meeting the twins was easy. Before reaching Petersburg, the D.D.S. had convinced the svelte blondes that the two extra bunks in his luxurious stateroom would be much more comfortable for them than sleeping on thin cushions placed inside a tent on the steel floor of the ship's solarium.

"My aging grandparents would be very happy if you took their bunk," Randazzle reassured the Scandinavians. "They wished desperately to make this cruise with me, but at the last minute their failing health kept them at home. I promised to send them pictures and to do my best to have a good time in their absence. You two can help make the old timers happy by sharing what was to be their evening quarters!"

How could the twins resist? The late afternoon already showed sporadic signs of nighttime stormy weather. They would be sleeping outside in a rainstorm at best and possibly, in an arctic gale at worst. In their innocent minds, Randazzle seemed more like a caring parent than the scheming voyeur that he really was.

"What could go wrong?" they rationalized. Convinced they could assuage his failing grandparent's concerns by keeping him company, and in addition, by supplying the old folks with pictures of their grandson along the journey, they enthusiastically agreed to the dentist's proposition.

Randazzle sniffed success. He innately discerned that he *"still had what women want."* He knew he was back in the hunt and was becoming increasingly overconfident with his talent and charm. His adrenaline flowed.

Yvonne and Yvette, enjoyed the overwhelming generosity of their new benefactor. They took pictures of him as the *Columbia* passed scenic mountains, waterfalls, logging and fishing outposts, lighthouses and other scenic sites along the cruise. So that all three could pose in the picture together, passersby often volunteered to snap photos with Randazzle's expensive Nikon zoom lens. With encouragement, the twins draped their lithe, young bodies around the excited old hustler in one sensual pose after another, often playing the tease to their new found sugar daddy.

The afternoon waned and started to turn to evening and Randazzle persuaded the giddy twins that they should dress semi-formal for dinner. During the hour and a half layover in the Petersburg port, he provided his American Express card for the beautiful debutantes to outfit themselves with elegant attire. They spent freely, each procuring a fashionable wardrobe for what promised to be an upscale evening on the ferry. No expense was spared.

With boxes and bags of hastily acquired clothing in hand, they hailed Petersburg's beat up local taxi cab and barely made it back to the ferry before the dock's doors closed. The departure horn sounded and soon the ferry again set sail toward Juneau.

Randazzle's senses were aroused and his nostrils flared as he escorted the twins back to his cabin to dress for the evening.

Dinner at the ferry restaurant was exquisite. Yvonne enjoyed Crab Louie and Yvette feasted on Scallops Mornay. True to form, Randazzle devoured a ten ounce New York steak, rare, with two orders of clams on the side for an aphrodisiac. All three cleansed their palates with Cabernet Sauvignon before finishing their meals with red velvet cake and vanilla bean ice cream.

Daylight quietly turned to twilight and a sense of romance lingered in the air. Leaving nothing to chance, Randazzle escorted his mesmerized guests to the cocktail lounge. The pianist was playing classical Mozart over the conversational buzz of his piano bar patrons. Champagne flowed freely as the aging barroom horndog continued to pick up the tab for the appreciative, jaw dropping twins.

All three clinged closely to one another, clutched arm-in-arm as they laughingly left the lounge to weave their way to the stateroom. Randazzle sensed victory.

...

Waking up late the next morning, the aging Arizona playboy was confused. His confusion turned to embarrassed anger when he discovered the ferry was docked in the Hoonah harbor and he was alone; curled up in a blanket on the hard floor of the stateroom. He had somehow slept through the Juneau layover and retained only a fuzzy recollection of the activities after leaving the piano bar the night before.

His Alaska fishing trip was about to commence and he instinctively recognized that his "sure thing" romantic interlude had somehow gone wrong. Looking around the room, he focused on a note taped to the mirror. It read:

"Dr. Randazzle, Thanks for a fun time! ...and thanks for the new outfits and warm, comfy beds. (Sorry you had to sleep on the floor!) After our vacation, we'll mail your cell phone, your maxed out credit cards and your wallet to your wife in Arizona. We hope you didn't get a headache from the sleeping pills we slipped into your champagne.

—LOVE YA LOTS! YVONNE AND YVETTE"

Angrily, Randazzle grabbed his fishing gear and disembarked the *Columbia*. He walked briskly until reaching a narrow, busy roadway that led to downtown Hoonah. He was in a hurried search for a way to get from Hoonah to the *Alaskan Bear Lodge*, which he learned was just a mere twenty five minutes across the Icy Strait.

Since he had missed making the planned connection with the other fishermen in Juneau, Randazzle felt pressured to find a way to the lodge so he could get himself back on schedule. He started waving at passing cars, hoping to hitch a ride with someone that could be of help to solve his dilemma.

The aging hustler felt older, but not much wiser. "At least," he rationalized, "I still have my Nikon camera and it holds plenty of evidence of my conquest with those detestable twins. My new fishing buddies will be impressed when they see my pictures!"

Once Randazzle came to terms with his predicament, he became practical. "I need to find a way to get to the lodge so I can get back on schedule and sort this mess out," he rationalized. "Without money or a cell phone, I'll have to apply my charm and common sense."

After the dentist disembarked the ferry and walked through the passenger loading and unloading lot, he was on Hoonah's Front Street. It was the busiest street in town and began at the Icy Strait Point Cannery on the north. The road then meandered southward past the ferry terminal, through town and past the Icy

Strait Lodge. Within a short distance thereafter, Front Street changed from a well maintained paved road into a gravel path which wound its way into an awe inspiring, tree filled countryside.

Hulme could see a cruise ship anchored in the harbor adjacent to the Cannery. He was not anticipating that he would also see half a dozen bright yellow and orange kayaks full of enthusiastic tourists, rowing their way across the harbor, but that was the scene playing out before him. Front Street's narrow two way road was bustling with activity and there was only a small road base shoulder for him to stand on without being too close to the traffic.

Randazzle assumed the position of a hitchhiker, squaring up with the street and sticking out his thumb. The first vehicle to pass was a white, late model twelve passenger tourist van. Even though it appeared to be overflowing with Asian sightseers, the driver slowed and pulled to the side of the road. He invited the hitchhiker to "get in! Wherever you're headed," the muscular chauffeur smiled, "I'm going that way, too."

The front rider's side seat was vacant, so the D.D.S. opened the door and hopped in, pulling his single piece of luggage behind him. He plopped the small travel case onto his lap.

"Welcome to Hoonalulu!" the driver laughed. "I'm taking cruise ship tourists on an exclusive tour, but you're invited to join us. My name's Keith Skaflestad."

Not wanting to run up a bill that he could not pay, the dentist introduced himself and replied "I don't have any money..."

Skaflestad laughed and replied, "Well, neither do I, so this should work out just fine!"

The burley driver then put on a microphone headset and pulled his van back onto the pavement. As he drove south on Front Street toward town, he began what sounded like a recorded travelogue. Enjoying himself and laughing loudly at his own jokes, he proceeded as if he was oblivious to the fact that his van was full of non-English speaking Asians who did not understand a word he was saying.

Nonplused, Keith drove through Hoonah pointing out what he considered to be the highlights. "Over there on your right is the post office and on your left, there, is the police station. Two of our three cops were shot and killed in a shootout last year. It's always something around here! If you go up this road and turn to the right, you'll be at the city dump. We won't be going up there, though, unless we have a hard time spotting some bears out in the country. The smart bears all go to the dump every afternoon for lunch, so if we don't see any out in the bush, I know where we can find 'em!"

He continued, "We have eight hundred people here in Hoonah and I'm related to around six hundred of them! My grandpa married a Tlingit and so did I, so I'm related to both the whites and the natives. Half of 'em love me and the other half hate me! Go figure."

Hoping to get to the fishing lodge on schedule, Randazzle told Keith of his predicament. "One way or another, I need to get over to Excursion Inlet, to the *Alaskan Bear Lodge*. I paid for a week of fishing, but somehow I slept through the layover in Juneau. Since I didn't get off the ferry there, I missed meeting my fishing group and ended up here in Hoonah. How can I get from here to Excursion?"

"I'll get you there," promised Skaflestad. "It isn't far from here. As soon as I'm finished with these customers from the cruise ship, I'll be heading across the Icy Strait to Excursion. I need to go up the Inlet to pull my crab cages, so I'll be going right past your lodge. I can drop you at their dock!"

"Whew," thought Randazzle. "This just might work out after all."

"Are you hungry?" asked Skaflestad. "I own a little cafe in town named Grandma Nina's and we make the best halibut tacos in Alaska. After I drop off these paying customers, we'll go have lunch!"

"Thanks. Yeah, I'm getting hungry. I can pay you when I get to the lodge and find a way to access my money. I've lost my wallet."

"Don't worry about that!" returned Skaflestad. "The money part always works out. You can earn your lunch by helping me pull my crab cages."

"The Hoonah tour should be over soon, since the town is so small," thought Randazzle. However, he did not expect that the tour included taking the tourists deep into Hoonah's outback to "see the bears."

Two hours later, Skaflestad turned Randazzle and the band of inscrutable tourists back towards town. (Thanks to the unpaved gravel roads, however, it seemed like much longer than two hours!) With no bear sightings on their expedition, which the guide suggested was "a rare occurrence!" they started toward the city dump to finish the tour on a high note. After observing Randazzle's tension beginning to mount, he concluded the Japanese guests would not care if he skipped the city dump portion of the tour.

To keep everyone's focus on bears, Skaflestad asked no one in particular, "Do any of you know the difference between a grizzly and a brown bear?" Forgetting that none of his guests spoke English, he surmised that the sea of oriental grins and blank stares could only mean that they hadn't a clue.

"The answer is about fifty-miles!" he laughed. "Grizzlies and brown bears are the same animal, but they're called brown bears if they're within fifty-miles of the ocean. Browns eat fish and grizzlies don't. Other than that, they are the same."

"Ok. Here's another one for you," he continued. "What animal family do the bears belong to?" Again, nothing but blank stares. "Jeeze, you people seem to have become disoriented, if you'll pardon the expression! Ok, I'll give you a hint: The females are called sows and the males are called boars. Now can you guess?" Still nothing but stares.

"Are you serious," Randazzle asked? "Bears are from the pig family?"

"Yep. Now, how can you tell the difference between the sows and the boars? ...other than the obvious way, I mean. Just by looking, can you tell?"

"No idea," Randazzle answered. "How?"

"The sows have a flat, pug nose and the boar's noses are long and pointed!"

"Well, I've learned something," Randazzle admitted. "Not to be pushy, but is this tour about to end? I need to get to Excursion."

"Yeah, we're almost done. I promised these folks they'd see bears, but I think they're happy just talking about them. They look pretty content as it is."

Everyone was relieved when the van was again on a well paved road once they entered the city limits. To bring his guests back into the conversation, Sakflestad put his headset back on and continued the verbal portion of his guided tour: "There on your right is the school. I was the varsity wrestling coach for a while; that is, until I had a fight with the principal and got myself canned." Again, he laughed at his joke and went on. "Ok, Dr. Randazzle, the bear tour is over. I'll run my guests back to the cruise ship and then we'll go have lunch at Grandma Nina's. Afterward, we'll board the *Karen-Marie* and go pull up some crab cages. When the day's crabbing is done, I'll get you to your fishing lodge."

Skaflestad carefully drove his van through downtown Hoonah, past Grandma Nina's Café and north toward the Icy Strait Point Cannery. As they motored along, Keith started cussing under his breath. "It's that damned officer Andy and he's got his red light on. He's pulling me over! What the hell? I've been going the speed limit. Damn it! He's harassing me again!"

With no room to pull over on the right side of the road, the guest filled tourist bus signaled left and pulled slowly into the compact Hoonah Trading Company parking lot. Alaska Wildlife Trooper Andy Torgensen followed closely behind and just to draw attention, pushed a button and emitted a short blast on the police car siren.

"What now, Andy?" Skaflestad asked incredulously. "You can't leave me alone, can you?"

"You need to come with me to Nugget Falls," Andy replied. "Right now!"

"I can't," Skaflestad replied sternly. "I have to finish my tour and I promised my friend here that I'd get him to Excursion. I can't leave right now."

"Give the keys to your friend, Keith. He can take your guests back to the cannery. You're coming with me, NOW! This is official *Brotherhood* business! You don't have a choice!"

Skaflestad gave Randazzle instructions to take the tourists back to the Cannery and told him to go to Grandma Nina's for a complimentary lunch. "Andy insists on taking me to Mendenhall Glacier in his chopper on some official business. He says we'll be back in a couple hours, so enjoy your lunch and feel free to drive around and get acquainted with Hoonah. Don't worry. I'll get you to your fishing lodge before dark."

Randazzle had no choice. When Skaflestad left in the trooper's vehicle, he confidently put on the headset and, in broken Japanese, told the confused orientals to "Shitoberuto o shimeru! Wareware wa, danpu ni mukatte iru!" ("Buckle up! We're headed to the dump!")

The Asians were ecstatic. "Kuma! Kamera wa junbi ga deki-mashita!" ("The bears! Get cameras ready!")

The van was filled with excitement as it left the Hoonah Trading Company parking lot and traveled toward the city dump. Guests were engaging with one another in animated conversation and frequently expressed themselves in bear attack charades, complete with the accompanying growling and menacing facial expressions. Randazzle's decision to complete the bear hunt had turned them into an even happier band of tourists, if that was possible.

As an afterthought, when they reached the center of town, Randazzle pulled into Grandma Nina's and ordered "Fish Tacos for everyone, compliments of Keith Skaflestad!" In a few minutes, they were back on the road with lunch and drinks in hand. They ate in merriment as their new guide drove toward the smoky hillside that identified the location of the dump. The van soon turned off Front Street and wound through a paved, forest lined lane leading to the landfill.

When the enthusiastic tourists rolled past the barrier gates, they were not disappointed. As promised, several bears were in their "natural habitat" foraging through the trash for lunch. Digital cameras of all shapes and sizes appeared and the excited patrons pointed and snapped picture after picture, all the while talking loudly to one another.

Their conversation was expressive, but not decipherable to the Alaskan who was standing at the back of his vehicle unloading trash. "Hell-o-mighty," mumbled the man as he finished pushing a pile of tree limbs out of the bed of his pickup. "They came all the way from Tokyo to take pictures of bears foraging in garbage. Tourism must be the business to be in these days."

While the event progressed, the sightseers felt an urgency to get out of the van to take better pictures. "What value is a bear photo if we're not in it?" they reasoned in their native language. Using multiple poses, they commenced to frame one another in photo after photo, taking pictures of the inquisitive bears at different angles in a myriad of snapshots.

After a few minutes and several hundred clicks of high tech Japanese cameras, the tourists had meandered to the north side of the dump. The van was parked on the south side and the bears had moved to the middle where two of them sensed an opportunity before any of the sightseers recognized the impending situation.

Two of the bears smelled the half eaten fish tacos and greasy wrappers that had been left on the seats of Skaflestad's van. Comically, they galloped single file in a serpentine path toward the vehicle. Once there, both bounded through the van's wide open sliding door and vigorously commenced eating the fish tacos.

Simultaneous with the bears' entry, Randazzle, who was the solitary occupant of the van, scrambled to get out through the driver's side door in a visible panic. "Skaflestad is going to kill me for this!" he shouted at the bears. "Get out of here!" The bears were not impressed. The sow was soon joined by her smaller cub, the larger one already enjoying his taco feast inside the twelve passenger.

In what was a matter of minutes (but seemed like an eternity), the bears had devoured the leftover food scraps. One at a time, they disembarked through the sliding door and bounded back to their original foraging spot on the landfill hillside. In shock, Randazzle and his gaggle of stunned onlookers made their way back to the van.

In addition to the ripping and, in some cases, the utter destruction of the Asian's backpacks, the van's seat covers were shredded and one seat was broken. Bear scat indiscriminately spotted the van with reeking aromatic proof that the demolition was not caused by human vandals.

Unexpectedly, Randazzle's debut as a tour guide was wildly popular with his guests. However, he knew he was in serious trouble with the tour company owner. The Asians had an exciting "Last Frontier" story to tell their friends and each of them rehearsed their personal version as the tattered vehicle slowly limped back to Hoonah.

CHAPTER THREE

PHINEAS POON

When Gary Liddiard deplaned Alaska Airlines on the Juneau tarmac, he had a sensation that he was stepping into an early springtime greenhouse. When the freshness of the atmosphere reached his senses, his first thought was that he was knocking on heaven's door. The mountain air was crisp and emitted a remarkably clean, rose garden aroma. The sky was deep blue with billowing white clouds that rolled gently through the Mendenhall Valley. Patches of misty haze oscillated gently close to earth.

Liddiard's visual senses were piqued beyond his expectations. The panorama included timber covered, snowcapped and sensationally steep mountains in every direction with waterfall after waterfall careening from jagged cliffs near the pinnacles, then cascading straight down in long, ribbon like flows. He was surprised that there were not just a few waterfalls; there were many.

As he rode in the taxi toward town, he enjoyed the beauty of the Gastineau Channel resting gently in the narrow valley between the majestic mountains on each side. When he neared the end of the ride, he marveled that there were five huge cruise ships docked tightly in the small downtown harbor. They each had the appearance of upscale, luxury hotels.

The pamphlet he was reading said the town was named for Joe Juneau, an early gold prospector. To him, the historic borough was reminiscent of some of the mining towns near his Sundance, Utah, home. He first remembered Eureka, western Utah's quaint old silver mining town from the late 1800's. As he pondered, though, he decided Juneau's ambiance reminded him more of Park City in the late sixties. The narrow, winding roads in both towns were festively lined with crowded, pastel colored, two story Victorian homes.

In the heart of Juneau's historic tourist district, as if all roads conspired to draw the retired Hollywood make-up artist to its swinging barroom doorstep, Gary left the taxi and entered the oldest man-made tourist attraction in town. He was at the turn of the century entry to the Red Dog Saloon.

The Red Dog prided itself as being Juneau's traditional gathering place for adventure seekers. The tourist trap, he noted as he walked through the swinging barroom doors, was a bawdy tavern. The place exuded Alaskan ambiance, in a dysfunctional sort of way.

On June 27, 1900, or so the legend goes, the notorious gunfighter Wyatt Earp checked his Smith and Wesson revolver at the U.S. Marshall's office in Juneau. Two days later, he boarded the S.S. Senator at 5:00 a.m., prior to the opening of the Marshall's office. Thus, his pistol was never claimed. Along with a mind numbing assortment of other artifacts, it hangs in a shadow box on the saloon wall for everyone to see.

According to Teri Tibett, a writer and musician living in Juneau, "when an elderly couple walks through the door of the Red

Dog Saloon in downtown Juneau, the first thing they do is look up at the stuffed black bear climbing the pole in the middle of the room and the stuffed butt of the man trying to get away from the bear. Or they see the mountain goat perched above the door or the seven foot painting of a sprawling naked lady hanging on the wall.

"Almost instantly, their good time is interrupted by a man over the microphone asking, "Can I help you sir? Do you have a reservation? Well, I have reservations about you!" Followed by a quip to the man's wife, "Oh, so you're with him now, eh?" They laugh and step in further. They're game.

"The man on the mic is Phineas Poon.

"Poon is one of four resident musicians performing during the summer at the world famous bar. He plays an old-style honky-tonk piano and favors turn-of-the-century tunes like the *"Maple Leaf Rag"* and *"Ain't She Sweet."*

"His show opens with background music played over the conversations of the people sitting at small round tables, drinking beer and chatting about their travels.

"Then, after a time they are greeted by the man on stage wearing a bowler hat, vest and garters on his sleeves.

"'Good afternoon! I'm Phineas Poon. Welcome to the Red Dog Saloon!"

"Poon immediately launches into "Oh Susanna" and at the end of each phrase, the piano stops and the audience sings out the last words in unison. They're hooked.

"The entertainer then leads them through a rendition of "My Bonnie Lies Over the Ocean" and the entire crowd raises their glasses above their heads swaying together and singing, "Bring back, bring back, oh bring back my Bonnie to me!"

"Now that he has their attention, he invites everyone to "play a dirty trick on the next person who walks in. I'll give you the cue. I'll say, 'Look who's here!' And I want you to give them a big

Alaska welcome. I want you to greet them like you haven't seen them in 30 years!" he tells the crowd of about 200.

"After a few minutes, another couple walks through the door and stops to shake off their umbrellas.

"'Look who's here!' calls Poon.

"The mob responds with loud cheers and hollers, applause and whistles. The couple, looking bewildered, steps back and decides to leave. They're not game.

"And the crowd laughs and carries on."

In the rarified atmosphere of Juneau's Red Dog Saloon, Gary found a seat near the piano bar and, as had been previously arranged, was soon joined by Captain Grantley Moore.

Phineas Poon (Tyler Dean "Tag" Eckles),
the Red Dog Saloon's notorious barroom entertainer.
Photo by David Sheakley of the Juneau Empire newspaper.

Ten minutes after Captain Moore was seated, Dusty O'Neal and T-Bone Jameson entered the swinging doors of the Red Dog Saloon. They were first startled and then pleasantly surprised by the welcome they received from the raucous crowd. Laughing and waving, they assumed the group had somehow been given advance notice of their arrival and were cheering their notoriety. But in reality, it was just funny business as usual at the Red Dog.

As was the *Alaskan Bear Lodge's* usual practice, Moore had been hired to be the group's fishing guide for the trip from Juneau to Excursion Inlet. Fishing was scheduled to start the following morning at 8:00 a.m., with the fishermen instructed to meet Captain Moore on the dock at nearby Auke Bay. The meeting at the Red Dog was arranged so the fishing group could meet the captain and organize for their following day's adventure. All were now present at the saloon, with the exception of the dentist from Arizona.

After the jeering from the crowd subsided, Liddiard waved the actors toward the two remaining empty seats at their small table. They enthusiastically greeted one another and joined in the usual "getting acquainted" small talk.

Hardly pausing at the end of his round of songs, Phineas motioned toward the group. "Everyone! Please give a big Red Dog welcome to an infamous sea captain and his unsavory crew," he dead panned loudly as he pointed toward Moore and his guests. The crowd, without a reason to celebrate the fishermen's notoriety other than the piano player's instructions, cheered and raised their beer mugs.

Poon continued, "These hardened sailors have come to Alaska from the ports of Eastern Russia, just to drink a mug of beer with YOU!" Again, the crowd cheered and toasted the four bewildered patrons. Being put on the spot, the fishermen also raised their glasses and joined in the toast.

After another animated round of songs, Phineas announced his intermission. He then flew off the small stage and pulled a nearby bar stool to the table, sitting between Liddiard and Moore.

"You guys are here a day early!" he exclaimed. "Luckily, I have the map and your directions with me. You weren't supposed to be here 'til tomorrow!"

"We're right on schedule," Moore finally managed while the rest of the men gazed incredulously at the entertainer.

"I must have my days mixed up, then," apologized Poon. "Here's your paperwork. Your instructions are on the back. I need to get back on stage, so I want you thugs to get the hell out'a my bar before someone recognizes you."

"Ha! There's already a good chance of that! You drew the crowd's attention to us a few minutes ago," Dusty reminded the entertainer.

"Well, I didn't expect you to show up today. It was unexpected... and in my confusion, spotlighting your table was a knee jerk reaction. Now, git yer crooked butts out'a here before I have you tossed out!"

With those threatening words, Poon returned to the stage and the bewildered quartet promptly exited through the swinging doors.

"What was that all about?" Gary asked Grantley as the group bunched together on the street corner. "I've never been thrown out of a bar before!"

"No idea," Grantley replied as he brushed off the incident. "Let's cross the street. We can eat lunch over at the Hangar Grill. Their coconut prawns are the best in Juneau. Besides, if Poon gave us a real treasure map," he laughed, "we can afford a couple extra servings!"

After being seated, Grantley rolled out the tattered and worn paper he had been given. "It's not exactly an old treasure map," he grinned. "It's more like a worn out advertising brochure for the Last Chance Gold Mine. The old mine is at the end of Basin Road, just a few miles up the canyon.

To make it easy for us, Phineas even circled a spot just above the mine museum. After lunch, we can drive up and scout out the place. Even if we don't find anything, you'll love it up there. The Last Chance is a step back into early Alaskan gold mining days."

"Sounds fun," nodded Dusty. "And I thought we were here just to go fishing!"

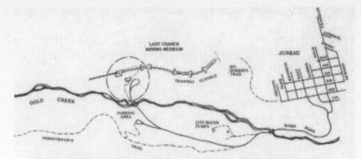

The Last Chance Mining Museum is the only historic mining building open to the public from Juneau's Gold Rush era. See the world's largest Ingersoll-Rand Air compressor, historic mining tools and equipment, minerals display, and the three dimensional "glass Map" of the Deep North ore body. Don't miss the "Alaska Juneau Adit," a unique underground exhibit of hard rock mining.

The Last Chance Mining Museum is operated by the Gastineau Channel Historical Society

CHAPTER FOUR

THE LAST CHANCE

Gold! Gold! Gold! Gold!
Bright and yellow, hard and cold,
Molten, graven, hammer'd, and roll'd,
Heavy to get, and light to hold;
Hoarded, barter'd, bought and sold,
Stolen, borrow'd, squander'd, doled,
Spurn'd by young, but hugg'd by old,
Price of many a crime untold;
Gold! Gold! Gold! Gold!*

—*FROM MISS KILMANSEGG AND HER PRECIOUS LEG"
BY THOMAS HOOD (1799-1845)

Leaving the Hangar Grill was not easy for the group. It took will power. The close up view of seaplanes landing and taking off in the water was mesmerizing and the coconut prawns were addictive. When the fishermen finally vacated the restaurant and loaded into Captain Moore's GMC Suburban, they were food drunk.

The drive through metropolitan Juneau, if indeed Juneau could be called metropolitan, took them past a small complex of state capital buildings and up the hillside, through an eclectic collection of well-kept Victorian homes. The turn of the century structures were built close to one another, with no side yards. As they are in all western mining towns, the fronts of the quaint buildings encroached onto the narrow streets.

The GMC motored along slowly on what eventually became a wooden plank road that cantilevered over the picturesque river below. The talk of gold mining made Tyrone excited about the prospects of finding gold.

"We get near a gold mine and you get gold fever!" quipped Gary as the young actor predicted the possibilities of gold panning success. "There were a lot of guys like you in the past that left this place with their tail between their legs... and with empty wallets!"

Winding through mature trees in the narrow flat bottoms of the canyon, they eventually came to a parking lot at the end of Basin Road. Signs pointed the way to the Last Chance Mining Museum, so they left the car and hiked across the narrow foot bridge spanning Gold Creek and then labored up an ascending dirt path. Halfway to their destination, the trail narrowed and then transformed into a steep zig-zag course, which was cut unevenly up the mountainside through the matured Alaskan forest.

When they reached the museum entrance, it was evident that something was wrong. Yellow crime scene tape fenced a "do-not-cross" barrier around the main building. Several somber looking officials wearing dark blue rain gear slickers were sporadically clustered in groups near the building. Large yellow letters across the back of their jackets identified their organization as the FBI.

The agents appeared to be gathering evidence from around the perimeter of the building and placing it in plastic garbage bags. The mood of the fishermen quickly changed to somber. No one spoke; but each looked at one another in uncomfortable surprise.

The curious anglers positioned themselves near the agents and engaged in conversation, asking them questions about the crime scene. With everyone focused on the dialog, Grantley and Dusty were able to slip past the group and continue hiking up the trail beyond the metal building until they reached the destination that had been circled on the tattered old map. They stood in the middle of a consortium of diminutive, old rusted out train cars that were scattered helter-skelter above the gold mine shafts.

Following Phineas Poon's sketchy directions, Moore slipped quietly through the doorway of the third car with Dusty following closely behind. The small compartment was claustrophobic and the atmosphere was pungent with the stench of rotting leaves.

Moore pushed debris away as he worked toward the farthest corner of the rusting boxcar. Once at the corner, he felt underfoot what he supposed was a small tree branch that was obscured under the covering of the decomposing leaves. Attempting to kick it away, he discovered it was the wooden handle of a miner's pick axe. Pulling the axe out of the leaves, Grantley was surprised to find that the forged iron head was still attached, so he began using the tool to scrape and claw into the ground. He began at the corner and methodically worked outward.

After making a clearing of several feet, they heard a metal-to-metal clunk. Quickly, Dusty knelt down and clawed with his hands until he was able to pull out a partially rusted metal box from under the rock and debris hiding place.

Using the mine pick, Grantley alternately pried and banged at the corners and edges of the box until the lid popped open. Inside the metal box, to their surprise, were eight well-weathered leather pouches. Scrawled across the top of each bag in black capital lettering, was what appeared to be the word "SNOOK."

Loosening the leather string that cinched together each bag's opening, the men's eyes widened when they saw what they estimated to be a king's ransom of pebble sized gold nuggets stuffed into each bag. "These nuggets must have been mined from the Last Chance Mine," mumbled Dusty.

After carefully transferring the pouches from the strongbox into his backpack, Grantley returned the empty box into the hole and then pushed and stacked rocks and debris on top of the dented container.

Exiting the derailed mining car, they retraced their steps back down the steep trail and stealthily merged back into the group. Everyone was intensely enthralled while they listened to the conversation between the mine curators and the FBI.

Gary Gillette was in mid-sentence as Moore and O'Neal reentered the group, explaining to the agents that for twenty years, he and Renee Hughes had taken care of the mine museum. He rehearsed that they had worked long, hard hours to recreate the site and restore the historic mining artifacts to their former glory.

Gillette further revealed that late Friday afternoon, shortly after the last of the tourists had left the building, he and Renee were surprised by a gang of rough looking Russian fishermen.

"At least," he explained, "they seemed to be Russian fishermen… their unkempt look, their accent… they all seemed to be Russians."

Interrupting her husband, Renee continued "one of the men held us hostage with a threatening sabre while the rest of them took lanterns and disappeared into the deteriorating mine shaft.

"Using picks and shovels they had taken from us, we could hear them digging not far from the mine entrance. The men eventually returned with a metal box they had apparently extracted inside the mine."

Gillette interjected, "They openly bragged to us that the box contained a fortune in gold nuggets."

"One of them," Renee frowned, "pulled old leather pouches from the box and scribbled something across each of them with a black marker."

After a short pause, her husband said, "When they attempted to take the box and its contents from the museum, Renee grabbed her cell phone and hit the speed dial. She connected with her friend, Phineas Poon, and frantically started begging him to send help.

"The thugs grabbed the phone and shouting Russian epithets into the receiver, they threatened Phineas' life as well as ours. Phineas was told, under no uncertain terms, that we would die if he didn't keep quiet.

"They told our friend that he'd be contacted with instructions, and if he valued his life and that of his friends, he'd better follow the directions! Under stress, Phineas promised he would comply."

"After the thugs scooped our gold samples and other valuables into my backpack," Renee explained, "my husband and I were strapped to the ancient mining machinery inside the museum. There, we languished over the weekend, unable to free ourselves. Fearing for our safety, Phineas must have decided to wait before calling the authorities. Luckily, Gary was finally able to free himself enough to untie me. After we got ourselves untied, we went down to the parking lot where we borrowed a cell phone from a hiker. That's when we called you."

The FBI said they had been on the trail of some Russian hooligans and thanks to Gillette and Hughes, they now had pretty good descriptions of them. The experience had taken its toll and emotions clearly showed on the weary and anguished faces of the two tired curators.

The fishermen collectively exhaled a sigh of relief when the FBI asked them to leave. Grantley and Dusty's minds were running wild

with the possibilities of what they could now afford and the lives they could lead with their unsavory gold nugget windfall. The FBI made no attempt to check Grantley's backpack or to search anyone in the group, for that matter. They left the Last Chance Mining Museum anxious to share the news of their ill-gotten discovery with their comrades. Their treasure map adventure had paid off handsomely and they were eager to inform Tyrone and Gary that they would all share in the windfall.

Gary Gillette and Renee Hughes. Last Chance Mining Museum curators.

CHAPTER FIVE

ELFIN COVE

When not engaged in its unique version of high seas
plunder, The *Rig* was often moored out of sight in an
obscure inlet off Cross Sound, a short distance from the
sheltered hamlet of Elfin Cove. Cross Sound was named by the early
explorer, James Cook, in 1778 because he found it on the third of
May, which was designated on his calendar as Holy Cross Day. Elfin

Cove, however, has no ties to anything
spiritual. In fact, the unpretentious
coastal burg has long been character-
ized as *a small drinking village with a
fishing problem*; and for good reason: it
is the known refuge of diverse bands of
latter-day pirates. The *Rig* is just one of
several commercial fishing vessels
belonging to a loosely knit society of
high seas marauders headquartered in
Elfin Cove.

While Quartermaster Dan Que Baxter busied himself oversee-ing the repair of a plank separation in the old ship's wooden hull, First Mate Jared Long cracked the whip on two of their Russian deck hands. Both men reveled in the absolute control they had over their mariner swabs.

The vodka induced stupor that had previously dimmed the minds of their ethnic galley slaves on that midnight binge in old Kamchatka had long since worn off and the young sea dogs were no longer happy with their semi-coerced decision to rejoin Cap'ting Snook and his motley crew.

"Avast, ye scurvy swabs! Pull down the riggin' on the aft sail," Baxter shouted upward to his understaffed and overworked boys. "Ye'd better 'ave th' sail mended a'fore Cap'ting Snook returns from his gamblin' party over at the Cove. Now, undress the bowline and bring down th' sail!"

After pilfering gambling funds from the captain's quarters, Bax-ter and Long instilled the age old fear of *"ye'll-be-walkin'-the-plank"* in the minds and hearts of their buccaneer understudies before they left to join Snook and the other gamesters in Elfin Cove. With a fifth of whiskey already consumed, the two men Snook had left in charge pushed the keel boat away from the *Rig* and were happily on their way to join their degenerate cronies for gambling, drinking, swashbuckler singing and high seas story telling.

Doctor Samuel Johnson once wrote, *"No man will be a sailor who has contrivance enough to get himself into a jail; for being in a ship is being in jail with the chance of being drowned... A man in jail has more room, better food, and commonly better company."*

In *The Pirate's Life at Sea*, C. Vallar went on to explain *"A mariner's life was anything but comfortable. He lived belowdecks in dim, cramped, and filthy quarters. Rats and cockroaches abounded in the bowels of the ship. Privacy was nonexistent, especially aboard a pirate ship where two hundred men might inhabit a world measuring one hundred twenty by forty feet... Bathroom facilities were primitive. Rotting provisions, bilge water, and unwashed bodies made the air rank. A storm meant days of dampness after it passed. Headroom between decks posed problems for taller men...*

"According to a sailor named Barrow, "There are no men under the sun that fare harder and get their living more hard and that are so abused on all sides as we poor seamen... so I could wish no young man to betake himself to this calling unless he had good friends to put him in place or supply his wants, for he shall find a great deal more to his sorrow than I have writ.

"Added to these problems were the dangers inherent in a sailor's life. He might plummet to his death while working the sails high above the deck. He might fall overboard, in which case the ship rarely returned for him and few sailors knew how to swim. Plus there was danger of fire or shipwreck. Also, the dull routine that was the norm between the sighting of sail and boarding a prize, numbed sailors' minds. Accidents and natural disasters certainly claimed sailors' lives, as did sea fights, but men were far more likely to succumb to disease than anything else. Scurvy, dysentery, tuberculosis, typhus, smallpox, malaria, and yellow fever killed half of all seamen.

"Drinking water, stored in kegs, turned foul and sailors were sometimes forced to drink this water. More often, though, they drank rum or grog rather than the brandy and wine that officers imbibed. Pirates, on the other hand, drank a mixture of rum, water, sugar, and nutmeg; rumfustian, which blended raw eggs with sugar, sherry, gin, and beer; and sherry, brandy, and port.

"The two most common foods sailors ate were salted meat and hard tack. The former might be kept in barrels for years before use. The latter was oftentimes infested with weevils."

Pulling down the mainsail was not an easy task for the two Russian teenagers. To offset their homesickness and desperation, in deep native accents they broke into the only sea faring song they knew. Laughing and singing loudly, albeit badly out of tune,

Yosif Kulavik and Boris Konovalov belted out the verses from an old turn of the century seaman folk song:

Come on the sloop John B.
My grandfather and me,
Round Nassau town we did roam;
Drinking all night, ve got in a fight,
Ve feel so break-up, ve vant to go home.

So h'ist up the John B. sails,
See how da mainsail set,
Send for da captain – shore, let me go home,
Let me go home, let me go home,
I feel so break-up, I vant to go home.

De poor cook he got fits,
Tro' 'way all de grits,
Den he took an' eat up all o' my corn!
Lemme go home, I vant to go home!
Dis is de worst trip since I been born!

"Yah, Yosif Kulavik," muttered Boris Konovalov in his deep guttural Slavic tone. "I vant to go home. Dis is de worst trip since I've been born!"

■ ■ ■

After six hours at the gaming tables in Elfin Cove, Long and Baxter were deeply engaged in what was starting to shape up as the all-night card game of their lives. Their small pouch of gold nuggets, seed money they had discreetly pilfered from the captain's quarters on the *Rig* earlier in the evening, had been enhanced with significant winnings. They were two of only five gamblers left in the game, the others having thrown in the towel as the evening proceeded. The other remaining card sharks were a trio from the Icy Strait: Johnny Crabill, Monte Mitchell, and Ponch Marchbanks.

All five punters were vying for the fee simple deed to the *Cove Lodge*, Elfin Cove's oldest sportfishing accommodation. Included in the pot was the former lodge owner's small fleet of sportfishing boats, including his personal prize: the *Rig* herself. The self-proclaimed terror of the Inside Passage had squandered his fortune on a game of chance. The disenfranchised former lodge owner, Sam McGee, had recently been eliminated from the game. His wealth and financial security were depleted by his senseless participation in a game in which he had very little skill. "The Bank" now legally owned the title to all of his Alaskan ocean side enterprises.

The trophy of his estate, at least in his mind, was the *Rig*. He had bonded emotionally with his old, worn out commercial fishing boat, even though the vessel had a growing reputation for being at the center of misdeeds in and around the Inside Passage.

In shame, McGee slunk angrily from the smoke filled casino, cussing the other gamblers. He also cussed the fickle deck of cards and, in general, cussed his now worthless life. As he disengaged, he bore the black cloud, downtrodden and broody appearance of a badly beaten, worn down and vengeful man.

The remaining gamblers were young, even though the evening was not. Earlier, at precisely 10:00 p.m., the *Coho's Bar and Grill* closed its doors to all non-gambling patrons. The tobacco reeking, make shift casino was filled exclusively with raucous, hardened fishermen. Each cankered soul huddled around the gaming table was intensely focused on confiscating the worldly possessions of the others. To a man, they raptly applied their less than elementary knowledge of the ancient game of Faro, while they simultaneously prayed for their fair share of Lady Luck. Each stared diligently into the eyes of the others for every opportunity to employ any underhanded stratagem that came to mind.

Ultimate ownership of the breathtaking gambling pot eventually narrowed to The Banker and the last remaining gambler: one of the saltiest of Alaska seamen, Jared Long.

"Fifteen and she goes," growled The Banker. The tension in the air grew thicker than before. An occasional loud sigh (and sometimes a moan) exuded from one or more of the onlookers.

Squinting through the smoke filled smog, Long maintained the hardened appearance of measured control as he bent the third corner of his card and ventured for fifteen times his stake.

"Thirty and she goes," The Banker entwined as he slid another card from the dealing box. Long turned the card downward to be used later, making it a fourth paroli.

"Sixty and she goes," heavily breathed The Banker. All eyes were fixated on First Mate Long. He stalled. "Sixty and she goes," repeated The Banker. Long ventured his all once more, then turned up the card he had saved.

There was silence, until in unison the entire gang of ruffians erupted into cheers. Jared Long was the new owner of the *Cove Lodge*, the *Rig* and all of the accompanying boats and equipment. With the gutsiest of hands, he had beaten The Bank!

While the party drank loudly to his success, without being observed by the inebriated patrons, the smoke filled room became engulfed in even more smoke. Smoke that was thicker, more intense and soon more suffocating than mere tobacco smoke. *The building was on fire!* Flames spread fast as the gamblers dashed to the narrow doorway, frantically searching for just one precious ounce of sweet, fresh air. Every soul desperately sought the relief that could only be found outside the building in the early morning sea breeze.

Suddenly, regretting his lightening retreat to atmospheric safety, Long reversed and returned toward the inferno that now engulfed the gambling table. He stubbornly scooped his winnings, including the lodge deed and boat titles, into his hat. Tightly holding the wealth from his night's conquest, he fell to the wooden plank floor and belly crawled in the direction he hoped was the *Coho* barroom door. Nothing was visible in any direction, except smoke! Nevertheless, he was unyielding in his dogged determination to secure financial liberty or death!

The timbers roared with the sizzling and crackling sounds of fire. From high above a truss beam dropped, crashing within inches of his head. Sensing his financial future was almost secure, the first mate doubled down his determination to safely exit the burning building. He loudly screamed a verbal contract with unseen and unnamed forces from the underworld if they would but help him escape the inferno with his health and his fortune intact. Finally, after what seemed to be an eternity, he felt the worn down wooden threshold and swiftly crawled to safety through the charred and sagging door opening.

Jared's eyes were burning and his eyesight was dim from his time in the smoldering haze. Regardless, he felt very little physical or mental discomfort. When any man hits the lottery, personal pain becomes inconsequential.

After exiting the flaming building and being able to again stand upright, Long roared the belly laughed of a pirate. Only he and his cohort in crime, Quartermaster Dan Baxter, stood to appreciate the irony from which he had appropriated Snook's worldly treasures. The Cap'ting was taken down by his own pilfered gold nuggets!

The following article appeared the next day in the *Juneau Empire Newspaper*:

FIRE DAMAGES COVE LODGE

A fire has heavily damaged a lodge and restaurant in the Southeast Alaska community of Elfin Cove.

Alaska State Troopers say the blaze, reported in the early morning, caused estimated damages in the $1.5 million range.

Troopers say the owners of the Cove Lodge woke up to heavy smoke in the kitchen and laundry area.

Elfin Cove firefighters and local residents unsuccessfully tried to put out the blaze. About 40 people made an assembly line to pass buckets of water from the beach to the lodge, an eyewitness told the Juneau Empire.

Other fire agencies from the region arrived later to help put out the fire.

The lodge and adjacent Coho's Bar and Grill sustained damage. The state fire marshal is investigating the cause of the blaze and troopers say no injuries have been reported.

■ ■ ■

Those forty some odd people that made an assembly line to pass buckets of water from the beach to *Coho's Bar*, did so in a vain attempt to douse the flames. The adjacent building, the *Cove Lodge* (not to be mistaken with the nearby *Elfin Cove Lodge)*, also became a casualty of the firestorm.

The state fire marshal's investigation did not turn up the ultimate cause of the fire. Although suspected by everyone, it was never proven that the fire was started by the distraught gambler who had wagered away his lucrative business and boats just a few hours before. It was speculated that Sam McGee set the fire to burn up his forfeited deeds and simultaneously end the lives of the "thieves" who had "cheated" him.

During the commotion that accompanied the fire, McGee slipped past the firefighting crowd, walked down the pier and disappeared into the early morning haze that surrounded the village.

In a hasty meeting of the town fathers the following day, the Elfin Cove Council outlawed the high stakes game of Faro and all other gambling vices. After the infamous inferno destroyed the *Cove Lodge* and *Coho's Bar and Grill*, the only game of chance still allowed in the picturesque fishing village is *"Go Fish."*

CHAPTER SIX

KUSHTAKA

The mood of the sport fishermen was mixed when they left the *Last Chance Mine*. No one in the group personally knew Gary Gillette or Renee Hughes, but all sensed the anguish both were suffering.

Grantley's hike from the museum back to the parking lot was a labored effort. "Lucky for us," he thought, "that the FBI had not observed the bulkiness of my backpack." During the initial hike from the parking lot to the mine, his backpack was empty and as flat as a pancake. On the return trip, however, it was bumpy and bulging at the seams.

Even though the FBI had failed to detect the change, Grantley noticed the difference. His load was significant enough to slow his step, but it was offset with his increased flow of adrenalin. He strained to make certain he hiked the trail with energy and did his best to walk with a normal stride.

When the group arrived at the GMC, Moore was perspiring and breathing heavily, as much or more from stress as from the physical exertion. He laughed it off when the others joked with him about his poor hiking conditioning. Nonetheless, their spirits were more than buoyed when they learned about the multiple sacks of gold in his backpack.

As each took their seat inside the Suburban, Grantley went to the rear of the vehicle. He opened the back door and hid his backpack behind the seat, placing a box of fishing tackle on top to obscure the pack from view.

"The gold needs to be kept out of sight, just in case we get pulled over," he informed the others. "We need to go somewhere out of the way until the dust settles and we're in the clear. There's so much wealth in those sacks that we'll all be on Easy Street!"

The GMC trailed down the canyon, crossed the wooden cantilevered section of road and then reentered Juneau. When they passed the capital building, Grantley had an idea. "Let's go see the Glacier," he cheerfully suggested to the others. "There's still time to get to Auk Ta Shaa. That's a place where no one will find us, even if they were looking. For around a hundred and fifty bucks, we can paddle a kayak across the lake and get close to the face of the glacier. That should give us time to think this out. It'll also give us time to be in the clear with the gold."

"I'm in," Tyrone volunteered. "With or without the gold, canoeing to the glacier is something I hoped to experience on this trip."

"Yeah. That's on my bucket list, too," Dusty agreed. "I read a brochure that said you can paddle right up to the icebergs and quite close to the waterfall, too."

Liddiard was not as enthusiastic. Seniors take longer to physically recover from mountain hikes and he thought canoeing across a frigid glacial lake sounded too much like work.

Grantley prodded him along. "You can do it easily and it's worth the effort. The three of us will do the heavy paddling. You just stick out your oar every once in a while and keep us from hitting an iceberg."

After receiving instructions in the outfitters cabin, Gary's confidence increased and he warmed to the idea. "It's beautiful out there," he observed. "If you young bucks are good for your word and I don't have to exert myself, then I'll join you for the canoe ride."

Once on the water, everyone was excited. The twenty eight-foot Tlingit-style canoe slid effortlessly and gracefully through the glacial milk surface of the lake, passing floating chunks of ice that had calved from the glacier. Unitedly, they paddled toward the bluish white glow of the majestic ice cliffs.

As they navigated the kayak past several icebergs, they were surprised to see such a wide variety of wildlife along the shoreline. They saw arctic terns nesting in the towering cliffs, as well as eagles, goats and even a bear and her cubs feasting on salmon remains that were snatched from an icy stream flowing into the lake.

The breathtaking solitude had a quiet, peaceful background noise that sounded somewhat like carbonated soda. Their tranquility was occasionally interrupted by blasts from fissures in the ice cliffs. The discharged cracking sounds were reminiscent of cannon shots.

"We're told to stay a safe distance from the cliffs to avoid being hit by a calving block of ice," Grantley instructed the group. "I know of a small beach just past Nugget Falls that's sufficiently hidden from the forest ranger's line of sight. We can get out of the kayak there and hike to a glacial cave behind the falls. You'll want to thank me later!"

When the team of kayakers passed the majestic waterfall, they found they had to shout toward each other to be heard above the roar of the cascading water. They were so close to the falls that they became damp from the freezing cold spray. Massive icebergs serenely floated past and were close enough for them to reach out and push themselves away with their paddles. They finally reached the shoreline Grantley had described earlier.

Nugget Falls at Mendenhall Galcier

After the kayak was beached, Dusty and Tyrone disembarked. Gary waived them off as Grantley stepped ashore and pushed the canoe back into the water. "Give us twenty minutes," Grantley screamed to Gary over the roar of the waterfall. "Then we'll meet you back here at this same spot."

Gary paddled the kayak back into the lake as the hikers, with their backpacks in hand, disappeared behind the falls. "In my younger days, I'd have been right there with them," he sighed to himself. "But not today! I'll just concentrate on keeping the canoe from capsizing!"

It was a short hike from the beach to the cavern entrance. A less experienced hiker would not have known that there was anything to see or experience behind the falls, but Grantley was a seasoned Alaskan and knew the secrets of Nugget Falls. Hiking over the top of a sizeable sedimentary rock and then squeezing between two more, the trio of adventurers finally stood in front of a well concealed cave entrance.

"Follow me!" Grantley's voice shrieked. His vocal chords had grown weak from screaming over the relentless roar of the deluge of water cascading between them and the lake. They shimmied, crawled and sliced through the difficult terrain until finally, to their audible relief, the crushing noise of the falls subsided after they entered a cavernous ice chamber that was hidden in the steep mountainside.

"Whew!" Dusty exclaimed, when all three were able to stand upright. "But what the heck is that smell?" It was a musk-like, dank and lingering aroma that was not unlike mildewed ammonia. However, the scent was slightly stronger than ammonia, in a black mold sort of way. The olfactory sensation was enough to snap the unlucky recipient's head backward and clear his sinuses at the same time.

As they passed further into the cave, they used the flashlight application on their cell phones to find their way while waiting for their eyes to grow accustom to the dark. Continuing cautiously, they inched further into the drizzling abyss. Suddenly, Tyrone stumbled over what appeared to be a ripped open backpack.

"What the..." he started to say. "It's someone's backpack. Look at this!" As his light illuminated the torn bag, he read aloud the barely legible name written on top: "Rob Durrans, M.D."

"Here's another one," exclaimed Dusty. "This one belonged to someone named Mark Warner." The second backpack was also shredded.

As they turned and looked back toward the cave entrance, they simultaneously discovered the source of the intensely disagreeable aroma they had encountered earlier. Lumbering from behind one of the huge rocks in the cavern and standing squarely in front of the small entrance was the biggest, shaggiest and most unfriendly looking beast they had ever imagined. The trio stood frozen for several moments.

"Kushtaka," Grantley finally managed to say as all three shrank in size and courage. "Sasquatch is alive and well and we're in trouble!"

Tlingit natives have passed down stories of Kushtaka from generation to generation. In some histories, the Sasquatch-like animal saves lost souls from what would surely be their frozen death by distracting them with illusions of family and friends and then transforming them into a fellow Kustaka, thus allowing the person to survive the cold.

However, in some legends, Kushtaka lures victims by imitating the cries of a baby or the screams of a woman. Once in his grasp, Kushtaka tears them to shreds, kills them or turns them into another Kushtaka.

Since Kushtaka mainly preys on small children, it has been said the legend was perpetuated by Tlingit mothers as a way to keep their children from wandering off and ending up too close to rivers or the ocean.

Having been raised in the Alaskan village of Tenakee Springs on Chichigof Island, Grantley was aware of all variations of Kustaka legends. From his youth, Tlingit elders had taught him about Kushtaka and he knew what the bulky beast craved.

Reaching slowly into his backpack, Moore pulled out several gold nuggets and skillfully rolled them near the animal's feet. With a broad smile, the creature gently leaned over and with a delicate stroke, picked up the gems. Repeating the drill, Grantley pulled out a few more yellow stones and, holding them in the palm of his extended hand, waived them slowly back and forth, tempting the beast to come toward him.

As Kushtaka slowly shuffled forward, Grantley tossed the stones and his backpack in the opposite direction. Kushtaka then trotted toward the treasure, leaving the entrance to the cavern unguarded. As if by telepathy, all three men dashed to the opening and helped jam each other through the small crevice and back into the daylight.

In a last second decision, T-bone grabbed what was left of one of the shredded backpacks and, along with his own, used it as a shield to ward off Kushtaka's grasping hand as he backed frantically through the exit. The beast could not follow since the aperture was too narrow for his large, hairy body.

"It was us or the gold and the gold wouldn't do us much good if we got torn to shreds," Grantley consoled his partners. "I wasn't about to lose my life just to be wealthy."

"But I liked being rich!" moaned T-Bone. "You're right, though. We're still alive. I'd like to figure out a way to recover the gold, but I won't be going back into that cave anytime soon!"

Dusty quickly concurred.

The fishermen concluded that there had to be a larger opening on the opposite side of the cave, one that was wide enough to allow Kushtaka to come and go from his concealed hideaway behind Nugget Falls.

When they were safely back in Juneau, Tyrone retrieved his iPhone and quickly typed a search request for Rob Durrans, M.D., the name that was written on the first shredded backpack. Finding a physician listed with the same name in Orem, Utah, he called the number to ascertain whether or not the doctor had escaped and survived.

Once the connection was made and the two briefly exchanged their common Alaskan experiences, Dr. Durrans promised to email details of what had happened in the cave to himself and Mark Warner. First, however, he obtained a sworn verbal commitment preventing Tyrone and his friends from disclosing what he called his *"farfetched tale."* He feared such outlandish and implausible details could damage his professional reputation with his patients and medical peers.

 Shortly after the telephone visit, the young actor received the following email from the Utah doc:

> Mark Warner and I swore an oath of secrecy to each other about our lost backpack adventure in Alaska. Knowing you are under oath to guard this sobering experience with secrecy, however, I will share our encounter with you in confidence.
>
> Last year, in August, Mark and I (along with our wives and a few family members) stopped in Juneau before heading to Excursion for five days of fishing. Like you, we rented a kayak from an outfitter in Auke Bay and went to explore the glacier up close.
>
> Not knowing there was a cave behind the waterfall, we explored the shore near the falls for a while before hiking across the face of Mendenhall Glacier to the west side. There, we found another beach and again went exploring.
>
> While everyone else in our group climbed to the top of the glacier, Warner and I were intrigued with the amazing caverns and passageways underneath the glacier. It was incredible...even magical. I can hardly describe the almost transparent deep blue ice walls, tunnels and swells carved into the bottom of that massive block of ice. I even have a picture hanging in my office that makes us appear to be enveloped inside a frozen wave of pristine blue water.
>
> We crawled, shimmed and slipped our way for half an hour in that surreal world, getting deeper and deeper under the millions of tons of ice. It was freaky - you can hear the glacier creaking, cracking, booming and groaning and you wonder if, at any second, it will suddenly move and entomb you in there forever.
>
> But it was the groaning that really spooked us!
>
> As we got deeper into the icy maze, the groaning got louder... or, closer, maybe??? We frequently gave each other questioning looks, but neither of us wanted to chicken out, so we just kept going.

After slithering on our bellies under a thirty or forty foot long ice shelf, we suddenly found ourselves in a fair-sized cavern. It was at least thirty by fifty feet with a ceiling sixty to seventy feet high.

We didn't need flashlights. At mid-day, the ice glows light blue from the overhead sun.

Four things happened at once: the groaning suddenly stopped; the stench of the cavern nearly made us lose our lunch; we noticed a couple dozen or more backpacks roughly piled in a heap; and finally, across the cavern sat a huge, dark animal staring at us!

My heart stopped beating as the matted, fur-covered behemoth never took its eyes off us... but continued chewing on something it had pulled from one of the backpacks. Neither Warner nor I could speak, but I knew if he attacked, I was a goner. Warner was closer to the entrance opening; ten years younger and eighty pounds lighter.

I did the only thing I could think of. Without taking my eyes off the beast, I slowly reached down and picked up my backpack. Quietly unzipping the main pocket, I took out a peanut butter and honey sandwich, pulled it out of the baggie and held it out in front of me as a peace offering, all-the-while, slowly inching my way towards him.

Warner whispered to me in a nervous, high-pitched tone "What are you doing???"

As I continued towards him, I realized the stench in the ice cave was the beast's breath. Now my stomach desperately wanted to empty its contents.

When I got within a few feet, I tore the sandwich in two and extended half towards the creature. We still had not taken our eyes off each other and, after a second, he reached out and took my offering.

When his paw touched my fingertips, I was surprised that it was warm. Somehow that made me feel slightly relaxed... although I was still beyond terrified.

Without hesitation, he stuffed the half sandwich into his mouth, chewed it up and grunted with contentment.

I took a bite of mine and somehow gagged it down.

We looked at each other for what seemed like hours, then he broke eye contact, reached into the backpack at his feet and pulled out a can of Spam.

With a grunt, he tore the package open; the spam sticking out of a ragged tin can while that gooey gel stuff dripped off of it. The monster grabbed the meat, devoured two thirds in a single bite, then held the rest in his filthy palm and again grunted as he extended his paw towards me.

What could I do? I hate Spam. Especially cold Spam.

He grunted yet again, this time with a little agitation in his voice, so I took a piece of whatever Spam is, and along with the monster's saliva dripping off of it, I nibbled a tiny bite from the side he had not eaten.

I'm not sure what happened next, except that he suddenly jumped to his feet and roared so loudly my ears are still ringing. He emitted a high pitched, three part whistle in a pattern of low-high-low. I was surprised the entire cave did not implode and crush us in a pile of glacier ice.

At that point, I lost it – literally – the combination of the smell in the cavern; ice cold Spam in my mouth; and the blast of his disgusting breath in my face, made me vomit.

I then spun around looking for Warner, but all I could see were the heels of his feet as he headed out to freedom.

Flying across the cave, I dove headfirst through the birth canal looking ice entrance and clawed my way out of there as fast as possible.

Not knowing if the beast would follow us, we ran - slipping and sliding, banging and bruising our way out, fearing for our lives.

I know we did not follow the same path going out that we did going in. I just kept screaming "GO! GO! GO!" and suddenly there was light and dry land ahead of us.

We scrambled out and quickly climbed upon some rocks – shaking like leaves – a little bruised and torn up, but still alive.

We sat there silently, just staring at the glacier and contemplating what had happened. I did not know what Mark was thinking, but I immediately knew no one would believe me if we ever told what had happened.

A short while later, the rest of our party returned. As we climbed gingerly into the canoe, my wife asked where my backpack was. I looked at Warner. He shot back a look of fear and shook his head "No!", so I told my wife it "fell into a crevice and I couldn't reach it. Warner verified that the same had happened to his as well."

We silently paddled back to Auke Bay, went to our motel and discreetly laundered our underwear.

■ ■ ■

Over what became the group's second and then third servings of coconut salmon hors d'oeuvres at the Twisted Fish Restaurant in downtown Juneau, Tyrone finished reading the doctor's email to the others.

To a man, they would never again be the same. Three were first person eye witnesses to a backwoods legend. After hearing Dr. Durrans' email, their aged, non-eyewitness colleague was finally convinced that his fishing buddies had told him the truth about the beast, as well as about the loss of their gold nugget fortune.

After Tyrone's reading of Dr. Durrans' email, Captain Moore gave instructions to his guests to meet him "in the morning at the Auke Bay Marina at seven hundred hours, appropriately dressed and ready to fish the Inside Passage from Juneau to Excursion Inlet."

Grantley then excused himself and slipped out of the restaurant through a side door. He was not seen again by anyone in the group until the following morning. The vacationers were more than ready to make the transition from being tourists into what they anticipated would be a more relaxed time as fishermen.

Nightfall's darkness comes gradually during the Alaskan summer. Gradually, that is to say, if it even comes at all. The eventide twilight lingers on after an elongated sundown, creating what becomes an unnerving extension of dusk that lasts well past midnight.

After arriving back at their B&B, Gary, Dusty and Tyrone felt the grayness hover, then settle on the mountains and descend slowly through the forest until finally falling onto Mother Earth. During the episode, they encountered lingering shrouds of mist surrounding the eerie, semi-darkened silhouettes that were shadowboxed by tall, old timber Sitka spruce in the background.

"Does Captain Moore seem a little cagey to you?" Ty asked Dusty, after he shuttered and shook off the reverie of the moment. "He stays in the shadows when we're in public and seems quite guarded whenever I ask about his family."

"I hadn't noticed," Dusty replied as he picked up a fishing lodge brochure he procured earlier at the inn's front desk. "In retrospect though, he sure seemed to be in a hurry to throw the pouches of gold away. It was almost as though it was rehearsed. But all-in-all, I'm okay with him. He did what he felt he had to do."

Looking up from the brochure, he asked Tyrone to hand him his backpack so he could compare the *Alaskan Bear Lodge* rates with those of the other lodge. After making comparisons, he smiled and said, "We got a very fair price at the lodge!" He smiled and held up the advertisements for Ty and Gary to compare for themselves.

Not interested in reviewing the brochures, Tyrone retrieved his backpack along with what was left of the shredded one he had used to shield himself from Kustaka. When picking up the damaged merchandise, he froze when he read the name dangling on the attached tag. It read *'Renee Hughes.'*

"Dusty! Call the FBI! ...here's the agent's card. This backpack belongs to the woman we met earlier today at the Last Chance Mining Museum! Since we no longer have the gold, at the very least, we should help them find the crooks that stole it in the first place."

Prior to the arrival of the FBI and the accompanying media, Dusty, Ty and Gary discussed the negative impact the actors' careers might suffer if they were labeled *"Bigfoot Eyewitnesses."* Since most Sasquatch encounters are made by folksy, uneducated red necks in back wood settings, they concluded it could quickly become an image problem for them.

As had Dr. Durrans and Mark Warner before them, the three made a pact to withhold any mention of the Kushtaka encounter. They also discussed the importance of remaining mum on the discovery of the pouches filled with gold nuggets. Since they had left the scene of the crime with the gold in their possession, it would surely become a legal issue for them. No one was anxious to be accused and arrested for being a thief or even an accessory to theft.

...

Greg Wilcoxsen, the agent in charge of Juneau's FBI Criminal Investigations Division field office, was first to arrive at the *Feather Bed*. Soon thereafter, a dozen more cars jammed into the parking lot. Included in the assemblage was an antique four by four Jeep, driven by Gary Gillette. His wife, Renee Hughes, was riding shotgun.

With notebook and pen in hand, beat reporter, Teri Tibbetts, busied herself asking questions on behalf of the *Juneau Empire* newspaper. In great haste, her assigned photographer, David Sheakley, diligently dashed about taking photos of everyone and everything that he considered to be remotely connected with the case. The communal sense lingering in the air was that the state capital's most recent high profile mystery was about to be solved.

As could be expected, the *Feather Bed's* patrons added to the confusion when they heard the growing commotion in the lobby. Up and down the hall, doors opened as guests cautiously peered out of their rooms. Eventually, still dressed in nightclothes, they joined the fray.

Agent Wilcoxsen, unaccustomed to such a mass of attention, found himself center stage as the backpack evidence was dumped onto a round dining table in the small hotel eating area.

"Yes, Agent Wilcoxsen," Dusty concluded toward the end of his interview. "We found Ms. Hughes' backpack wedged in some rocks behind the falls at Mendenhall Lake. We were surprised that it was thoroughly shredded and in such bad condition. I'm guessing it might've been the work of a black bear."

"That's how it appears to me as well," the agent-in-charge agreed. "I hope the backpack will somehow shed light on the location of the Russians. They must have been in the cavern yesterday. If a bear shredded the backpack, he might also have done the same to our suspects. We'll send some men to the falls to take a look around. I'll keep what remains of the backpack and its contents in the bureau's evidence locker. If anything develops, I'll call to keep you informed."

"Thanks for getting this evidence to the authorities," interjected Gillette. "Even though it's unsettling to retrieve it in this condition, at least we're finding clues to follow the trail of those thugs."

Grandma's Feather Bed

The crowd slowly dispersed as the three fishermen retired to their rooms. The old-timer of the trio went right to bed and enjoyed a night of sound sleep. The actors occupied the remainder of their evening treating their wounds and recovering from the scraping, scratching and bruising trauma they suffered while making their rapid escape from the ice cavern. Their conversation dwelt on how their adrenalin had masked the aches and pains of the minor injuries and how pronounced the trauma had become once they experienced an adrenalin letdown. Together in quiet solitude, they suffered the aftermath that made them feel like they had been in a train wreck.

Wanting to dull the pain, Dusty picked up the turn-of-the-century style guesthouse phone. "Hello, room service? Do you have some Tylenol PM available? ...and some gauze and ace bandages? My buddy and I got pretty banged up on our hike today."

Luckily, the quaint accommodations at the Victorian inn included vintage cast iron bathtubs. After applying the ointment delivered by room service, they spent several hours soaking in their respective tubs, hoping the soreness would eventually subside.

When the actors finished toweling off, gauze and bandages were carefully wrapped and both retired for the evening. However, due to the excitement of the day and the seasonal lack of darkness outside, neither was able to sleep deeply. Each tossed and turned in bed, imagining what could possibly happen next on their already eventful Alaskan fishing trip.

CHAPTER SEVEN

THE EQUINOX

Monday morning came early for the fishermen. The *Feather Bed* shuttle brought the adventurers and their luggage to Auke Bay, where Captain Moore was patiently waiting at the pier runway that led to the dock. His catamaran, the *Equinox*, was tied to the dock, positioned and ready for the passengers to on-load supplies and equipment. Stowage began, with everyone working as a single unit to safely

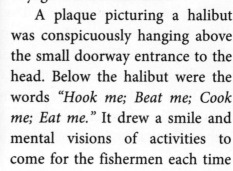

secure their goods for the fishing voyage to Excursion Inlet.

A plaque picturing a halibut was conspicuously hanging above the small doorway entrance to the head. Below the halibut were the words *"Hook me; Beat me; Cook me; Eat me."* It drew a smile and mental visions of activities to come for the fishermen each time they passed by while stacking the boxes of supplies in the compartments beneath the catamaran cabin seats.

Another well placed plaque, quoting John Steinbeck, read *"It has always been my private conviction that any man who pits his intelligence against a fish and loses has it coming."* The challenge had been made and, to a man, it was non-verbally accepted.

When the last of the supplies were loaded onto the *Equinox,* it became painfully aware to everyone that Dusty was showing signs of becoming squeamish about extended time on board a seafaring vessel.

"How long is this trip going to take and how far out to sea will we go?" he asked Grantley. Were it not for the look of anguish and apprehension on his face, the others would have continued their good natured ridicule and ribbing. It was evident, however, that Dusty had not spent much time at sea. The revelation was an interesting paradox for a man of his worldly experiences.

"Don't tell me you're nervous, Dusty!" quipped Gary. "How have you survived on those luxury cruises you've been telling us about?"

"Those don't count," Dusty sheepishly grinned. "Cruises are on big ships. Comparatively, this is a small boat and there are significant safety differences. Bouncing around on the open water on a boat this size scares the daylights out of me! I once memorized a pretty good poem, just for the purpose of avoiding a boating part in a movie scene. The poem's humor got the attention of the directors and I got sympathy. Lucky for me, my stunt double got the call to do the scene. After reciting my poem, I got out of bobbing around on that little dinghy!"

"Then let's hear a few verses, you coward!" insisted Gary. The group gathered around as Dusty stood on the dock, one foot perched stoically on a tie-off piling, as he recited:

THE LANDLUBBER'S TOAST
By Thomas Russell Ybarra

'Tis pleasant to taste of the spray
As the waters dash over the rail.
To be frozen and wet
And extremely upset
In the teeth of a thundering gale.

But the joys of a seafaring life
Are naught but the emptiest boast,
As glasses we clink
In a room that can't sink
And delightedly drink
A new toast:

Oh, here's to the land, yo ho!
Drain, drain every foaming tankard,
Oh, here's to the sea
As it looks to me
From a beach that is firmly anchored.

Oh, here's to the quiet, respectable street
Where the winds never howl
And the waves never beat,
Where the ground has been trained
To stick close to your feet, –
A health to the land, yo ho!

Yes, here's to the land
Where you stick to your chairs,
Where the beds do not fire you out unawares,
Where you know which is down,
And which is upstairs–
A health to the land, yo ho!

"Damn!" exclaimed Grantley in disgust. "Is this going to be another one of those panty waist voyages?"

"Ha! You're all suckers!" Dusty laughed. "You gullible little fishes jumped right into my net! I'm game to go anywhere you can float this bucket of bolts, *so let's shove off!* Let's get out of the harbor and go fishing before some second-rate bum pulls out that world record King salmon with my name on it!"

"Wait a minute... stop!" Grantley gravely demanded. He started waiving his hand toward a hearse-led funeral procession winding slowly along the narrow highway and across the bridge above the marina.

The captain took off his hat and held it firmly over his heart as he stood at rigid attention. The others could not help but notice a tear welling up in the corner of his right eye.

When the funeral procession finally passed, he took a deep breath, wiped his eyes and stood at ease. Dusty commented solemnly, "Grantley. I'm impressed to see that you are so sentimental."

Grantley stoically replied, "It was the least I could do. After all, for the past fifteen years I was married to the woman in the hearse. *Now let's go fishing, boys!*"

With howls of boyish whoops, they untied and shoved away from the pier, laughing the boisterous belly laughs of a band of men about to enjoy a well-deserved seafaring adventure.

• • •

All five senses were exercised when the energized fishermen exited Auke Bay. O'Neal, Jameson and Liddiard smelled the rich aroma of fish entrails that, for over a century, had been thrown from the decks of commercial fishing boats into the harbor waters.

They heard the constant *"Caw! Caw!"* of predatory birds as they dove downward to pluck their early morning breakfast from the discarded viscera. They felt the fresh coldness of the sea mist as the *Equinox* picked up speed after reaching the open waters beyond the "no wake" rules of the harbor. Their lips tasted the salty brine from the ocean spray that splashed thinly in the air as the ship's hull sliced smoothly through the waves.

Auke Bay

Mostly, though, they saw the immenseness and beauty of the Creator's handiwork all around them: the majestic, snow-capped mountains surrounding the valley; the steep, deeply carved canyons created by centuries of eroding waterfalls that endlessly cascaded from the mountaintops to the sea below; the dense forest covering of old growth, mature Sitka spruce; and the bluish-white hue inside the flowing majesty of the Mendenhall Glacier.

Man's creations gave accent and color to God's. There was a myriad of colorful ships, vessels and boats of all sizes, styles and uses tied to the docks in the harbor. There were colorful buildings strewn along the shoreline and dotting the mountainside.

The small coastal highway took the appearance of a curving, flowing ribbon that wound parallel to the beach, between the mountains and the sea. The appreciative fishermen enjoyed their moments of serene beauty and, in unison, simultaneously felt a shiver of wonder as they experienced unspoken reverence and respect for the grand awesomeness of it all.

Once in the open sea and comfortably cruising at thirty knots on a west by southwest course, Captain Moore steered the *Equinox* toward the Lynn Canal. He felt he could relax and enjoy the moment himself as he began pointing to the emerging sea life.

Pods of humpback whales were sighted off in the distance and he described their system of submerging and swimming back to the surface in a circular motion, in a team effort with other whales. Their synchronized collaboration created bubbles that served to confuse the krill, plankton and other small fish, rendering them easy prey for the whales to eat.

When asked to get closer to the humpbacks for a better photo opportunity, Grantley quietly replied "you really don't want to get too close. If they are feeding, they might unintentionally surface under the boat. It doesn't happen often, but when it does, it ends in disaster! Trust me on that one. I know from personal experience!"

Schools of orca (also known as killer whales) swam close by, as did porpoises, seals and all other manner of sea life. Arctic birds, including the colorful puffin (Alaska's state bird), were sighted. There was no end to nature's beauty and the variation of sightseeing enjoyment.

The sport fishermen were then given a rare glimpse into Grantley's personal history. He was born in Australia and his family migrated to Alaska when he was almost eight years old. As the family neared their new home in a small seaside village on the shores of the Icy Strait, their boat was capsized by a surfacing humpback whale. It was the very disaster he had just warned his guests about and they could see the sadness in his eyes when he finished the story.

His parents and twin brother, Samuel, were lost and presumed drowned. Even though all efforts were made, their bodies were never recovered. Grantley survived the sea by hanging tightly to a pine plank that had detached from the boat in the accident.

Frantically, he paddled toward land but eventually lost consciousness from hypothermia. Fortunately, a Tlingit fishermen sighted him, canoed to his rescue and saved him from a certain watery grave.

Nearby Chicagof Island elders revived and adopted him as one of their own. They raised him to manhood in the small village of Tenakee Springs. From a young age, he learned their tribal traditions, including how to fish and live off the land. Over time, Grantley became a fully adopted Tlingit son.

Always anticipating he would someday find his parents and brother alive, Grantley became a sportfishing guide. He migrated from one coastal town to another along the Inside Passage, hoping that his family would miraculously turn up. His faith and spirits were lifted on the occasions when, at random times and in random places, a fisherman or seaside merchant insisted they had met him before. Those encounters concluded that someone had come by that looked just like him. "A dead ringer," they often said. It was a dreadful saying that sent shivers up and down his spine whenever it was uttered.

Grantley established his reputation as an influence for good among the salty and often uneducated seafaring men who lived along the Alaskan shores. He was well known from Sitka on the south to Skagway on the north, as well as in the small towns and villages that dotted the shoreline up and down the Inside Passage.

There was not a better whale watching guide or sportfishing skipper to be found along the Icy Strait than Captain Grantley Moore and there was not a fishing vessel that was better outfitted than his *Equinox*.

CHAPTER EIGHT

THE SOLSTICE

Once the *Equinox* cruised past Point Defiance, Captain Moore slowed to a two knot troll. Quickly and expertly, he baited three hooks and, one at a time, put the trio of fishing poles on down riggers and reeled them out to specific distances from the boat. Within minutes of extending the lines, he enthusiastically yelled *"fish on!"* and his guests were instructed to grab their poles and start reeling.

All three fishing poles were bouncing and bent to their limits. The Coho were running and the seasoned captain had placed his exhilarated band of anglers dead center, right on top of a migrating school of salmon. All joined in animated shouts and pats on the back as three impressive Silvers were reeled in, netted and brought into the boat.

As soon as the fish were bled, another vessel - one virtually identical to the *Equinox* - eased up alongside the excited fishermen. "Mornin' gents. Permission to come aboard," rasped the gangly, sun leathered and unshaven fisherman from the other boat. "Permission granted," Captain Moore cautiously replied. Gary was instructed to steady and hold the two boats safely apart from one another as the two captains carefully became acquainted.

"I'm from Elfin Cove an' m' name's Sam McGee," the visitor volunteered. "But me sea farin' mates call me Cap'ting. Ah couldn't help but seein' the name o' yer boat. Quite th' coincidence t' have a pair a matchin' cat'merans, with th' one bein' named *Equinox* and th' other *Solstice!*"

With only a few minor differences, the boats were mirror images of one another. Moore's craft was outfitted for sportfishing and McGee's was laden to the hilt with commercial fishing gear. Another contrast was that the *Equinox* was tidy and well kept, while the *Solstice* was a sloppy, unkempt nightmare from top-to-bottom. It was obvious to all that it had not been cleaned for a long time, if ever. Fishing gear was strewn and piled everywhere, along with towels, beer cans and every manner of boat related equipment parts.

The contrasting physical appearance and general hygiene of the two captains was just as striking a disparity as were the twin catamarans. In fact, aside from both men being tall, lanky and similar in coloring, their oppositeness bordered on the comical.

Grantley was well kept and his reddish-blonde beard was short and well-trimmed. McGee, to the contrary, presented the look of a wild man. His long, matted auburn hair and beard, along with his filthy, wrinkled and torn clothing, were visibly apparent, even from a distance. Close up, his accompanying smell was reminiscent of a bucket of week old fish that had been left to ripening in the sun. His aroma was further enhanced by the head snapping, nasal clearing stench of what seemed to be the result of forest fire smoke.

Sam McGee, presented the appearance and aura of a homeless and forgotten soul instead of that of a boat captain.

When McGee opened his mouth to talk, the stench of alcohol mixed with rotted whiffs of odor from his cavity destructed, yellow teeth (at least, the teeth that were still in place) made his nauseated audience instantly draw back in self-defense. His salty vocabulary mirrored his appearance and smell.

Most noticeable of all his idiosyncracies, however, were a worn out eyepatch covering his left eye and an anchor tattoo on his left forearm. McGee exhibited the appearance of a very poorly costumed movie pirate.

The rag-tag Cap'ting's vocabulary was continually laced with profanity. His fractionated words and improper sentence structure sharply contrasted with Moore's educationally superior refinement. In every way, other than size and coloring, the two were the additive inverse of the other.

"How's 'bout a couple o' yer boys t' come fish w' me fer a'while," queried McGee. "I've got plenty a beer on ice an' they might larn a thing 'er two 'bout fishin' on my commercial rig. We kin fish north wilst ye's go t' th' south."

Making eye contact, Dusty and Tyrone both indicated their mutual interest in exploring the possibility of an alcoholic diversion, mixed with the probability of enjoying a high seas adventure. Moore's boat had thus far proven to be "dry" and they entertained no hope that Liddiard, a Utah Mormon, would have any hidden spirits stashed in his duffle bag.

Jameson had stowed a flask of whiskey in his backpack and O'Neal had retained most of a bottle of Johnny Walker Red in his. Nevertheless, both had been concerned that they would have to horde their libations for later in the week. They were encouraged that McGee indicated that he had plenty of beer on his boat.

"Let's give it a try!" T-Bone smiled. "This trip is about adventure, right?"

While Gary continued to steady the *Solstice* and keep it from bumping the *Equinox*, the two movie stars hopped aboard. Both were eager for the possibilities of a commercial fishing adventure. McGee followed quickly.

"We'll meet you at the lodge later tonight," yelled Dusty as the *Solstice* powered up and pulled away.

"Fifty bucks says we'll bring home the most fish today!" barked Tyrone, in a challenge to both Gary and Grantley.

The *Equinox's* remaining fisherman and her captain stared at each other in amazement. Moore finally re-engaged his mind as well as his trolling motor.

"What in hell are those two thinking?" Grantley muttered aloud. "Men and fish are alike... they both get into trouble when they open their mouth!"

"Yep," replied Gary. "Offer a pair of play actors a beer and they're hell-bent to jump ship and ride off with the devil himself!"

When their southwesterly course stabilized, Moore and Liddiard put out their fishing poles and once again found success trolling along the Chatham Strait shoreline. Dusty and Tyrone, on the other hand, discovered that their plate held much more than they had bargained for.

As soon as they were out of sight from the *Equinox,* McGee slowed the *Solstice* to a two knot troll. The unsuspecting fishermen had each downed an ice cold Coors and were pulling the tab off a second can when the Cap'ting locked his boat into a steady course. He sat stiffly on the edge of an upside down water bucket and pulled a large knife from a scabbard that had been holstered in his thick belt.

Securing a sharpening stone from the boat's stowage shelf, he began honing the menacing looking blade. *"Whet, whet, whet."* The sound of the metal slicing against the stone was uncomfortably riveting. *"Whet, whet, whet."*

The actors soon found themselves partially entranced, partially frightened and completely immobilized. "That's quite the machete you've got there, Captain McGee!" Dusty finally managed.

The seasoned seaman raised his eyebrows but not his head and momentarily stared at his guests. With the swift motion of an assassin, he raised the saber and with a brisk blow, sliced the head off of a Coho lying on a nearby box. Then, as if nothing had happened, went back to filing his already razor sharp knife.

"Whet, whet, whet." Tyrone winced.

"Whet, whet, whet." Dusty stiffened. Both suspended from movement.

"Y'd best git this hell hole swabbed 'n spit shined!" growled McGee. "...b'fore yer heads 'er rollin' 'round on th' deck wi' that dam'd ol' fish!"

"Crrraaaaap," muttered Tyrone quietly without moving his lips. "We're on board with a madman!"

"Whet, whet, whet."

Finally, Dusty broke the silence. "Ty, hand me that water hose over there. Let's get this ship cleaned up. Where are we headed, Captain?"

"Juneau! We're goin' to m' gold mine. I need t' replenish th' fortune I lost last night. I've got some bags a gold stashed over there. One uv m' sorry, damn'd shipmates cheated me at Faro an' stole away m' lodge an' boats over in Elfin. I need t' git some gold t' buy 'em back! You two volunteers'll be doin' m' heavy liftin'! ...an' frum here on out, ya best call me by my seafarin' name! Out here on th' water, ya' don't me Sam. Here, I'm respect'd an' go by th' name uv Cap'ting Snook. I'm feared 'cross the Icy Strait and clear over to th' eastern shores uv Mother Russia!"

Both actors looked at one another as if a light had turned on in their brain and they stiffened in horror as Snook's identity sunk into their consciousness.

"Whet, whet, whet."

"Hey, boy!" Snook stared directly at Tyrone. "See th' paper nailed to th' wall over there?" He pointed his sword, touching the tip of it to a sun weathered, wind torn parchment. "I wanna' hear a good readin' 'o that verse!"

Ty carefully pulled the paper from where it was nailed to the wall and glanced over the rough hand written page. It was four verses from Longfellow's "*Wreck of the Hesperus.*"

"Are you serious?" he asked in earnest.

"Serious az dried blood on a knife," Snook replied. "Read it good 'n ye won't git cut! We're sail'n in dangerous waters, don't ya' know!" Snook then pressed the point of his knife to Tyrone's throat and held it there. "Read it fer me, actor... jist fer luck! Lyrics are th' pirate's way o' prayin', don't ya' know?"

Ty promptly began to read from Longfellow's poem. With a knife at his throat, he read with conviction. To further satisfy Snook, he added the throaty accent of a pirate:

And ever the fitful gusts between
A sound came from the land;
It was the sound of the trampling surf,
On the rocks and hard sea-sand.

The breakers were right beneath her bows,
She drifted a dreary wreck,
And a whooping billow swept the crew
Like icicles from her deck.

She struck where the white and fleecy waves
Looked soft as carded wool,
But the cruel rocks, they gored her side
Like the horns of an angry bull.

Her rattling shrouds, all sheathed in ice,
With the masts went by the board;
Like a vessel of glass, she stove and sank,
Ho! ho! the breakers roared!

"See that rocky shore over there?," Snook bellowed. "It's th' Vanderbilt Reef an' many hunderts o' people died in a shipwreck on that reef. You two jest might join 'em if'in I decide t' toss y' over board. So, if'n y' lousy landlubbers don't buck up an' do az I sez, I'll strap ye both to th' sides of the *Solstice*... but it won't be fer yer safety. I'll be usin' ya 'fer bumpers t' perteckt m' hull frum the rocks! Then, when we're back t' calmer seas, I'll be a cuttin' ya loose t' let y' plunge into th' freezin' waters an' y'll hafta' sink 'er swim."

A long fishing day in Alaska is decidedly longer than a long day fishing down in the lower forty eight. The sun never seems to set. It just lingers at the edge of the sky.

O'Neal and Jameson labored for what seemed to be many over-time hours. They strained to pull in the long outrigger fishing lines and then unhook the salmon. Repeatedly, they resent freshly baited hooks back down into the water to catch more fish. Their fingers became so cold from exposure to the icy water, they feared they might discover that one or more of their digits had snapped cleanly off of their hand.

Intermittently, Snook returned to his less than subtle task of sharpening his long knife on the whet stone. He interspersed the *"whet, whet, whet"* sharpening sound with his well measured snarling and the barking of demands to the cringing fishermen.

During a brief lull in the action, Dusty hatched a scheme: "I'd like to try my hand at Faro," he said to Snook. "In the new *Wyatt Earp* movie that is about to be released, T-Bone and I cleaned up Old Tucson. Ty played the part of Doc Holliday and I played Wyatt. I made a living running a saloon Faro table before the shootout at the OK Corral and I got pretty good at Faro. I'd be interested in a game or two with you to find out if I'm any good in a real game."

"Y' don't have anything to wager," sneered Snook.

"We could put up some of our royalties from *Wyatt Earp*," suggested Tyrone.

Dusty replied, "Are you nuts, T-Bone? That's a lot of money. I'd ever do anything that stupid!"

The conversation suddenly piqued Snook's attention. "What's in yer backpacks, boys? We might be able t' start a Faro game w' sumpin' small."

"I have a flask of whiskey and O'Neal has what's left of a bottle of Johnny Walker Red," Tyrone suggested.

"Ha! I'll jest take the booze frum ya'. Why should I even bother to wager?"

"Because you're a man," Dusty patronized. "And you want to get your manhood back after that trouncing you took in Elfin Cove! I'm an amateur at card games, so this might be the day your luck turns for the better!"

"Break out th' cards," Snook grumbled. "Put yer booze on th' table 'n I'll wager m' knife aginst it. I kin bust both a' ya with m' bare hands anyways. I don't need a knife t' hold ye."

The table was set up and Tyrone was instructed to hold "The Bank," which now consisted of two bottles of alcohol and the Cap'ting's razor sharp dagger, which he sheathed snugly in a well-worn scabbard.

The game went quickly and Snook was soon sipping from his newly won whiskey flask.

"Once more," Dusty begged. "I'll get the hang of this game and be better competition for you. I'll even put up one percent of my *Earp* royalties if you'll put everything back in the pot! ...including your knife," he added as an afterthought.

Staring at his opponent, Snook reopened the flask and downed its remaining contents. After a pause, his whole body shivered from head to toe and he expressed a heartfelt "aaaaaggghhhh" when the heat from the alcohol finally settled in his stomach.

"Some sez th' flask iz half empty," he philosophized. "I jest sez give me what's left an' I'll finish er off!" Snook laughed loud and long at his joke.

"Th' wager'll be fer ten persint frum both a yer royalties! ...an' y'll be abettin' fer m' knife and two empty bottles. Take 'er or leave 'er! We'll need a proper signed contract, though. It hasta' be writ up legal an' witness'd, an' all that. Otherwise, no bet!"

"Then you'll have to throw in some poles and fishing gear, just to make it fair!" countered Dusty.

"Write up th' damn contract," a confident Snook ordered. "I'm in!"

Tyrone wrote the compact on the reverse side of the worn out paper containing the verses from Longfellow's poem. All parties signed and Jameson signed as the witness. The Faro game was on once again, but this time with greater stakes. Wagers between the two gamblers went back and forth until it was evident that the pot had to be increased to proceed any further.

"Raise th' percent!" Snook suggested sternly.

"Not unless you put up something of value... that's a legally binding contract you made me sign and I won't gamble away my income without a chance for something of value!"

"How 'bout the *Solstice*? Up it t' fi'ty persint each on yer royalties an' I'll wager the *Solstice*!"

Visibly loopy from the alcohol, McGee pushed on: "An' it'll all hav' t' be added t' th' contract; sign'd an' witness'd... an' all that!"

Dusty hesitated. After a visible sigh, he and Tyrone finally relented. "Ok. We're in if you are, but for fifty percent you'll have to put up the title to the boat *and* everything on it... including the fish!"

"Done!" shouted the Captain. "Write 'er up, banker. An' both a ya' prepare t' lose yer royalties!"

When McGee looked down at the paper while signing the agreement, Dusty smiled a half smile and winked assurance to Tyrone. With pursed lips, Jameson nodded back his acknowledgment.

"Shuffle the cards, Captain," Tyrone insisted as he slid the deck toward the bobbing gambler. The bottles were completely empty and the spirits had taken their toll.

Three quick hands later, the *Solstice* had a new owner. In addition to the fully equipped commercial fishing boat, the actors also took ownership of the razor sharp sword with its scabbard, two empty whisky containers and a good sized fish hold filled with salmon. The Captain quickly sobered.

"Ya' lousy landlubbers! Ya' cheat'd me!" He continued to scream, curse and threaten the two men until physical violence was imminent. When he grabbed Tyrone by the throat in a fierce death grasp, Dusty pulled the knife from the scabbard.

"I'll cut you in half and feed you to the fish!" Dusty threatened. The knife drew blood on the Captain's right wrist, causing him to withdraw his grip on Tyrone's carotid artery. As he pulled back, he stumbled and Dusty quickly jumped on top of him, placing the knife at his throat.

"If you even move, I'll slit your throat!" he warned.

McGee cowered, knowing the strength from Dusty's adrenaline could end his life in less than a second. "Stop!" he shouted. "Stop! I surrender to ya'. Y've got me dead t' rights!"

"Step onto this bucket," shouted Ty as he shoved the white plastic water bucket Snook had used as his whetting chair. When the Cap'ting hesitantly complied, Jameson instantly hit him with a forearm shiver and pushed him with a mighty shove. McGee toppled over the side of the boat and fell screaming into the freezing waters of the Lynn Canal.

"I think you have less than ten minutes to make shore before hypothermia gets you," Dusty yelled over the side.

"I'd jump in and help you," sneered Tyrone, his neck still throbbing from Snook's choking grip. "But I just finished a sandwich and my mom taught me to wait half an hour after lunch before going for a swim!"

"Your mom's right, T-Bone!" Dusty cautioned. "Best do as she says!"

After watching Snook struggle in the water, Dusty laughed as he said to Ty, "I love playing Faro! All those hands we played night and day on the *Wyatt Earp* set made us masters. Snook didn't stand a chance. Just like Wyatt and Doc, we let him win the first few hands, just to get the ante up and the contracts signed."

"This was a lot more fun than any of those games on the set," Tyrone grinned.

Dusty then turned the *Solstice* south, and at forty knots, they barreled full speed in the direction of the lodge. Off in the distance, they watched an angry and drenched pirate safely reach the dangerously treacherous rocks of the Vanderbilt Reef.

An hour later, as the waves gently beat against the twin catamaran hulls of the *Solstice*, Tyrone and Dusty sat quietly on water buckets trolling for salmon and drinking Snook's ice cold beer. The GPS identified the beach as Home Shore and they knew that in a few more miles, they would be within sight of the *Alaskan Bear Lodge*.

Softly, as if to avoid frightening away the fish, T-Bone muttered "I think I'm going to divorce my wife. She hasn't spoken to me for over two months."

Dusty continued sipping his beer and thoughtfully replied, "If that's your only complaint, buddy, you'd better think it over. Women like that are hard to find!"

They both enjoyed the humor as well as their breathtaking surroundings. Mostly, however, they enjoyed reeling in one giant fish after another on what was now their very own, legally deeded commercial fishing boat.

CHAPTER NINE

SWEET CHEEKS

Meanwhile, back in Elfin Cove, Ponch Marchbanks and his gambling associates were exhausted after their vain attempt to extinguish the fire that ultimately destroyed the *Cove Lodge* and *Coho's Bar and Grill*. Two of the village's landmark properties had been lost and neither had the benefit of fire insurance coverage. Both were reduced to nothing more than an ashen pile of smoldering rubble. It was a sad morning for everyone in the hamlet.

The Icy Strait contingent was in agreement that it was time to head home and sleep away the nightmare that had become their new reality, so Ponch left his friends to retrieve his boat for the journey home. He became livid after he walked down the dock and discovered it was missing. Having tied the *Solstice* to the pier near *Fish Masters Inn*, he knew his boat could not have just floated away. Someone had taken it.

Ponch searched up and down the Elfin Cove boardwalk until he found Jerry Sheldon, the owner of *Fish Masters*. Jerry was the person most likely to shed light on the boat's disappearance.

"The last guy I saw on the dock was Sam McGee," Jerry said. "It was about the same time that all hell broke loose up the hill at *Coho's.* "I have no idea what he was doing, but he sure looked agitated. When the fire alarm sounded, I passed in a hurry, almost knocking him down. He swore a blue streak at me, but hell, that's just Sam."

"Keep an eye out for my boat, will you, Jerry? I'll see if I can hitch a ride home with someone headed in the direction of Gustavus. I'm tired to the bone and ready to sleep off this all night party."

Johnny Crabill, Monte Mitchell and Bruce Gordon, the boys from Excursion Inlet, consented to return home by way of Gustavus to help Ponch get home. Since they were tired, they were not enthusiastic about adding extra boat time. However, it was not too far out of their way and Alaskans are known as being willing to help other Alaskans. Besides, Ponch was the leader of their local fraternity and because of that common interest, they had developed a long time bond with one another.

To a man, they were very tired. All were covered with smudge and soot and smelled deeply of pungent, sinus torturing smoke. Not that they were anti-social, but no one had an interest in sitting close together on the boat ride home. The mood was somber, but at least the water was smooth as they traveled through Cross Sound and then entered the sometimes choppy waters of the Icy Strait.

Crabill's thirty two foot aluminum fishing boat, the *Crab Daddy,* cruised effortlessly at thirty two knots, thereby allowing them to reach Gustavus in less than an hour's time on the open water. From the monotony of the ride and the humming of the motors, all four men were semi-comatose when they arrived at Gustavus's recently improved dock. The group disembarked together, ascended to the top of the pier and hiked a little over a mile along the narrow road to the *Angler Inn.* Their unified hope was to recharge their energy with a cup of hot coffee at the Inn's small café.

After warming themselves by the fireplace and getting a much needed caffeine boost, Johnny, Monte and Bruce returned to the *Crab Daddy*. Ponch walked to the side street near the Inn where he had parked his relic of a vehicle the day he left for Elfin Cove.

Initially, Ponch's beat up old pickup was unwilling to start, but after cranking the engine over and over, the spark finally ignited. The motor sporadically coughed and wheezed as blue smoke poured out of the exhaust. Throwing caution to the wind, he steered his dilapidated Ford down the well-worn, pot hole riveted dirt road that lead to his cabin.

Once inside his home, Ponch collapsed fully clothed, reeking from head to toe from forest-fire-strength smoke and soot. It was early afternoon when he partially awoke from his deep, snore laced unconsciousness. The phone was ringing off the hook and had been doing so for three or four minutes. Reaching blindly in the direction of the noise, in a sleep induced stupor, he clumsily knocked the phone off the end table. Fumbling, he grasped the handset and responded to the raspy voice on the other end. "Take it easy, Sammy. I've been sleepin'. Other than your losin' yer fishin' lodge in that Faro game last night, what're you so worked up about? You sound like the devil his-self!"

Following a long pause, Ponch erupted into the phone: "Damn you, McGee! How could you gamble away my boat? The *Solstice* wasn't yours to gamble away, you jackass... you sold it to me two months ago and you didn't even have my permission to take it. You're a damned thief! I had to hitch a ride to get home from Elfin last night. Where the hell are you, anyway?"

After hearing McGee's shaky apologies and the explanation as to where he was, Marchbanks lit into him again. "I'll get my seaplane out'a the hangar and come pick you up. You'd better hope the water's calm enough t' land the ol' crate, or we're both sunk! Watch the skies for me and make sure I can find you. Build a fire on the beach! Damn you, Sam! Double damn you!"

Marchbanks was fuming. Ironically, he smelled like he was fuming. Not taking time to shower or change to fresh clothing, he grabbed his faded *"Big Butts-Sweet Cheeks"* flying cap and pulled it tightly onto his balding head. He rushed out the door and sprinted to his private airplane hangar.

The archaic seaplane had not been fired up since the preceding summer, so Ponch was forced to dig deeply into his bush pilot bag of tricks to get the propeller to catch. After nearly reaching physical exhaustion, the old master finally got the motor to sputter and the prop began to whirl. The engaged engine, however, sounded much the same as his beat up pickup. Coughing, wheezing and blowing blue smoke, the rusted out Cessna U206, which was ingloriously held together with duct tape, lurched out of the hangar and quickly lifted off the ground.

Ponch cleared the Sitka spruce surrounding his narrow makeshift airstrip with only a few yards to spare. It was a close call, even for a bush pilot with his expertise. He exhaled a long, loud sigh of relief, trimmed his gear and headed toward the rugged and rocky Lynn Canal shoreline.

While in flight to rescue McGee, Ponch pondered ideas to set in motion a scheme to recover his catamaran. His mind raced and his confusion was exacerbated by the constant clanking noise from the engine of his ancient aircraft.

The legendary *Sweet Cheeks* seaplane was in the air and on yet another treacherous rescue mission. It was unclear as to whether the smoke streaming behind the maroon flying contraption was coming from the untuned, antiquated equipment or from the fuming aviator himself. It was probably from both.

• • •

The Alaskan experience combines natural beauty with unique manmade accents. The landscape, sea creatures and wildlife defy description. In addition to the eclectic personalities of the natives and the ongoing revolving door of immigrants, man's contribution to the scenic Alaskan shorelines include the towns and villages as well as the remote, back country lodges and cabins. All of these structures add to the broad and diverse ambiance found throughout the forty ninth state.

In and around Excursion Inlet, the water is mirror-like and pristine; the snowcapped mountain ranges are majestic and are enhanced with innumerable cascading waterfalls. From the right vantage point, there is good visibility of a distant receding glacier in the Fairweather Mountains. All manner of fowl and sea life are active and in constant view.

Boats, ships and barges travel to and from the Ocean Beauty Cannery, just a mile or so north from the mouth of the Inlet. They come to sell freshly caught fish, replenish their fuel tanks or to cruise the Inlet to enjoy its beauty.

At the mouth of Excursion Inlet, as if standing sentry, is the *Alaskan Bear Lodge*. Devin McMichaels is the lodge keeper, as well as the handyman, outfitter, chief cook and bottle washer. On this blue sky afternoon, he rested lazily on a reclining wooden chair that was perched on the deck of the lodge's sea wall, reveling in his daily dose of "me" time.

As he did each Monday, he found time to drink in the fresh salt flavored air while awaiting the arrival of another new round of midsummer fishing guests. With leisure time nearing an end, he was enjoying the last few hours of solitude before his next wave of guests arrived. Intermittently, when he found the energy to do so, McMichaels left his state of reverie and returned indoors. There, he continued to organize the lodge and restore everything to tip-top condition. Beds still needed refreshing and toiletries had to be set out.

Lunch was nearing completion and required attention. Devin's signature crab cakes and his other freshly caught, locally prepared delicacies, were spread tastefully on the lodge bar. He knew it was the calm before the storm: a weekly occurrence at every fishing lodge in Alaska; one that took place just prior to the time when the week's new guests arrive.

Off in the distance, the fit, red haired innkeeper could see a white speck gliding into the distant Hoonah harbor, on the opposite shores of the Icy Strait. It was yet another cruise ship filled with tourists and he knew from experience that his cell service would now become spotty. Inexplicably, cruise ship passengers simultaneously exhibit a need to use their cell phone each time they reach a new port. Presumably, the excitement of disembarking at such a scenic, native Alaskan town as Hoonah, impel them to call friends and relatives back home. Whatever the reason, the mass of concurrent conversations max out the Hoonah cell tower and render phone users across the water at Excursion Inlet with little or no cell phone access.

Doc Warner's Alaska Fishing Adventures, an iconic lodge just south of Devin's *Alaskan Bear Lodge*, has been providing non-guided fishing opportunities since 1981. Employing the aid of his binoculars, McMichaels watched the horizon. He was studying the activity aboard a *Doc Warner* fishing boat, which was anchored between two of the nearby Porpoise Islands.

A fisherman on the aluminum craft had just reeled in a medium sized halibut and his fishing partner was mercilessly whacking the fish between the eyes with the end of a gaff while the happy angler busied himself attaching new bait to the oversized halibut hook. *"Big Butts-Sweet Cheeks,"* Devin smiled to himself.

It is well known in Alaska that the cheeks on big halibut are the sweetest meat on the fish. "The bigger the halibut, the sweeter the cheeks," he though out loud.

McMichaels turned his binoculars slightly northward to scan the deep blue outline of the Fairweather Mountains and the iridescent blue-white glow of the Fairweather Glacier. No matter how often he repeated this exercise, he found it to be emotionally fulfilling.

A bald eagle flew across his spy glass vision and he watched intently as it swooped gracefully to the water, extracting a Dolly Varden trout with its mighty talons. The bird returned to the top of a nearby spruce to share the fresh lunch with his mate. Gently, a soft breeze blew a low hanging cloud of mist further up the inlet; simultaneously, it refreshed the seaside air surrounding the lodge and, as breezes do, refreshed and recharged the lodge keeper.

Devin's nature induced trance was briefly interrupted when he heard the sputtering and coughing of what he recognized as Ponch Marchbanks' worn out sea plane.

"I wonder where Ponch is headed this afternoon," Devin thought out loud. "One of these days, ol' *Sweet Cheeks* isn't going to make it. He should tune up that rusty bucket or we'll be fishin' the venerable old coot and his contraption out of the deep... or even worse, we'll be peeling them both off the side of a mountain!"

McMichaels watched and then waived his hat as Marchbanks flew dangerously low overhead, dipping his wings from side to side in acknowledgment of his friend's salute. Blowing blue smoke, the old Cessna and its seasoned bush pilot banked sharply to the south and steeply gained elevation. There was little room to spare when he turned eastward and flew over the mountain at South Pass.

"I hope he makes it," Devin thought out loud. "I hope *Sweet Cheeks* doesn't clip a wing today. In that old crate, it's not 'if', it's 'when.' It's just a matter of time, but today is just too nice of a day to spoil with a plane crash!"

Trolling at two knots along the shoreline directly beneath the maroon seaplane, Devin sighted Captain Moore and the *Equinox*. "Right on time," he thought. "I'd best get a hustle on and put the finishing touches on lunch. The boys'll be hungry."

Ten minutes later, the *Equinox* carefully pulled to the lodge's floating dock and Devin reappeared on the porch. He was surprised to see only one of his four expected guests.

After being introduced to Gary, he asked "Where are the actors and the dentist?" The answer he received was gruff and abbreviated. "Those damned actors left us and went on another boat and the dentist never even showed up!" Gary grabbed his backpack and went inside to explore the lodge while the captain and the lodge keeper hauled the suitcases and fly fishing gear from the *Equinox* to the lodge.

When the fishermen's bags were secured, Grantley went back to his boat and pulled a freshly caught salmon out of the hatch. With seasoned confidence, he proceeded to filet the catch.

"Here's the fillets from a couple Pinks we caught down by the *Salmon Run*," he smiled. "Put 'em on the barbie while they're fresh and they'll taste just as good as Silvers!"

Devin put the fillets in a bucket and took them to his kitchen. He agreed with Grantley's opinion about the less appreciated "Humpies" and took the fish to the smoker to prepare for lunch.

The trio was almost finished eating their seafood lunch when the *Solstice* quietly and gently pulled up to the dock behind the *Equinox*. After a hasty tie down, the actors-turned-commercial-fishermen moved quickly toward the dinner table. They were visibly excited and impatient, wanting to share their story of adventure and intrigue with their captive audience.

Early on, McMichaels, Liddiard and Moore brushed off Dusty's over-enthusiastic tale and labeled it as pure fabrication. To verify their claims, Tyrone hastily retreated to the *Solstice* and returned waiving the signed and witnessed legal documents above his head. After reviewing the deeds and statements, the trio of listeners were convinced.

While Dusty recited the sequence about Cap'ting McGee getting knocked down and forced overboard at the tip of his own dagger, Liddiard laughed so hard he felt tears running down his leg. At least, he thought it was tears.

Following lunch, the men sorted through their fishing gear while they listened to the lodge keeper's stories. Devin was a master storyteller and he intertwined fishing strategies and boating lessons between his tall tales.

When the boats were organized and ready for action, they took a cruise to the top of the inlet, passing both South and North Creek and the Ocean Beauty Cannery in the process. On the return trip, they stopped at the cannery dock, hiked up the pier stairway and walked the boardwalk toward the small grocery store.

The small village consisted of several old military barracks, which were all painted white. One of the long, low buildings had been converted into a grocery store, so they entered and went in to get acquainted. After purchasing a few fishing lures and devouring an ice cream bar, they toured the cannery's quaint historical museum. Thereafter, they returned to the dock and boated quietly back to the lodge.

Sleeping quarters were assigned and the small group of fatigued fishermen crawled into their beds, anxious to get the rest necessary to arise early for the following day's fishing. They were exhausted.

Dusty and Ty retired to the upper floor and settled in the north bedroom. In the absence of the dentist that was scheduled to be his roommate, Gary retired alone to the upper south bedroom. Both sleeping rooms were conveniently situated adjacent to the tackle and outfitting loft, which served as an additional rest and relaxation area for lodge guests.

Gary was bone-tired and was well beyond ready for a good night's sleep. He climbed the ladder and crawled quietly into the top berth of the comfortable bunk bed, snuggled the down comforter up to his chin and was snoring loudly within a matter of minutes.

Hours later, towards early morning, he was awakened by a noise. Carefully leaning over the mattress to look down from his top bunk perch, the fisherman was surprised to see an unidentified occupant sitting atop the covers on the lower berth. Excepting himself, the room was empty when he had fallen asleep the preceding evening and he was startled to find that he had a roommate. A very ghastly looking roommate.

The stranger sitting on the edge of the bed clutched an old style fishing rod in one hand and held an odd assortment of outdated, worn and tattered fishing gear in the other. His hair was disheveled. He had a wild eyed stare and exhibited what appeared to be a severe case of the shakes. His demeanor was reminiscent of a frightened fugitive on the lam.

Gary remained quiet and was hardly breathing. All the while, he thought it was possible that he was about to become the victim of a lunatic. At last he arose, slid noiselessly over the edge of the bunk and onto the floor. Aside from the shakes, the unwanted roommate did not move. Liddiard opened the door slowly and crossed through the tackle room. He tacitly went down the spiral staircase and entered the great room below. Once safe and feeling secure on the main level, Gary paused and breathed his first full breath of air since initially seeing the intruder.

Devin was the only other person in the lodge who was awake at that early hour and was busy in the pantry preparing the ingredients for the upcoming breakfast. Noticing Gary in the great room, McMichaels discerned that his guest was visibly shaken. After a moment, he unwittingly became an eyewitness to the cause for concern. Standing at stiff attention, both men watched Gary's erstwhile roommate ungracefully descended down the spiral staircase and, with a noisy thump, pause to rest on the main floor landing.

The dark and disturbed looking personage was clad from top to bottom with ragged *Mossy Oak* camouflaged underwear. The only covering over his filthy undergarments was a dirty, sleeveless night shirt with a threadbare image of an old fashioned fishing fly over the embroidered inscription "Bite Me."

The fishing rod continued to shake wildly in his hand as he stared at Devin and Gary, both of whom stood frozen in their tracks. The lost soul then sauntered slowly to the door of the lodge, looking all the while over his shoulder at his captive audience. He haltingly opened the door, then turned and leered as he looked at the men. It seemed to be a very long minute for Devin and Gary. Listlessly, the lost soul then disappeared into the thick morning fog.

Gary's voice was no more than a rasping whisper when he informed the lodge keeper that he was intensely stressed from the experience. He said he felt as if his racing heart was about to explode with anxiety. Incoherently, he rambled on to his sympathetic listener until summarizing that from past experiences, he "had a deep fear of drunken vagrants."

"Based on descriptions I have been given from others," McMichaels replied, "he's not a drunken vagrant. What we just saw was a Tlingit apparition who has turned up at random places around these parts for almost a century. The ghoul, so the legend goes, forebodes good stream fishing. He's said to be an ancient Excursion Inlet native who fished up and down South Creek, just below Lake Neva. When the Army took over Excursion and turned it into a military base, and later a prison camp, it's said that he appeared in the barracks each year when the Sockeye start to run.

"To immortalize this apparition, as well as to show their appreciation, some of the military men built an impressive cement post entrance on the Lake Neva road. It's still there, at the head of the trail leading to the most productive fishing hole on South Creek.

"Trust me, the lodge was locked up tight last night. But as ghouls do, he somehow got inside. I've heard that's how it always is. After being discovered, he leaves as quickly as he came and then dissipates into the night. There is never a conversation or anything. It's inexplicable. Of course, when he's gone, it's a relief to everyone. The apparition isn't dangerous. He's just a ghostly figure. The good news for us, though, is that we now know the sockeye are running at South Creek!"

Awakened by the wafting aroma of sausage, eggs and hot coffee, Dusty and Tyrone joined Devin and Gary in the kitchen. "Where are we fishing today?" asked Dusty.

"South Creek," Gary answered with a half-smile. "Apparently, the sockeye are running!"

CHAPTER TEN

GLACIER BAY

After winning ownership of the *Cove Lodge* and its fishing boats, Jared wrapped up his business in Elfin Cove and returned to the *Rig* with Dan Baxter. The lodge had been reduced to a smoldering pile of ashen rubble and he discovered that the lodge's most completely outfitted fishing boat, the *Solstice*, was not owned by Snook. Since selling it to Ponch, he occasionally rented it. The two other lodge boats were satisfactory for local fishing, but not adequate in size for commercial fishing. The best asset that Long won in the card game was the *Rig*.

After negotiating wages, Baxter agreed to continue employment as the *Rig's* first mate. Long, as the new owner, took on the title of captain and assumed the mantle of officer-in-charge.

Under Long's command, the morale on board went from bad to worse. With his "inner pit bull" raging out of control, he verbally abused what was left of his reluctant crew. Finally, albeit at the point of his sword, the men fell into line. From his demeanor, they were convinced he would delight in killing them... if for no other reason than just to see them kick.

Long ordered Baxter to have the men pull anchor and quietly leave the obscure cove, located part way between Elfin Cove and Pelican at Lisianski Inlet. The *Rig* set sail through Cross Sound, passing South Inian Pass and barely missed hitting Million Dollar Rock. (The treacherously narrow passage got its name because of the cost of ship wreck damage the partially hidden reefs had created over the years.) They traveled past Lemesurier Island and, in due course, found themselves cruising in the open waters of the Icy Strait.

Once they were inside the bottleneck entrance to the Icy Strait, Glacier Bay cell towers provided improved cell service and Captain Long was able to connect with Ponch Marchbanks. Finding that Marchbanks and Snook were together, he sought ideas for improving his ship. Even though Snook was no longer the titled owner, he was relieved to know the *Rig* was being moved to a different location and that Long was willing to let him remain associated with the old boat he had long revered.

Snook's sense of loss was further mitigated when Jared accepted his plea to join in designing a plot to help him and Ponch recover the *Solstice*. Using Ponch's cell phone, Snook suggested that Jared bring the *Rig* into the protected waters of Glacier Bay where she could be docked close to Ponch's warehouse.

"Materials 'n equipment are more readily available at that location," he proposed. "Since th' lodge at Glacier Bay is remodelin', we kin git all kinds a wood 'n material that they're gonna throw out.

"Ponch's homestead is jest a few miles upstream frum Bartlett Cove and not far from th' pier," he continued. "We'll want the *Rig* az close az we kin git it t' Ponch's tool shop."

After Jared agreed, Snook disconnected and asked Ponch to call ahead to secure the obligatory permission to dock the *Rig* at the wharf near the *Glacier Bay Lodge*. Since he was well known in Gustavus and to those who ran the lodge, it was easy for Ponch to make connections and succeed in getting an ideal spot where they could tie down for repairs.

The Park Service personnel especially liked the suggestion that the *Rig's* crew would haul out the discarded material from the lodge's renovation. They knew they could save money and effort by having Ponch salvage the items he wanted.

Upon arrival, the *Rig* docked and tied to the farthest corner of the pier, as far out of sight as possible from curious onlookers. In such a setting, the old ship appeared to be just another obsolete vessel in the process of being refurbished. Visually, the boat was long overdue for patching, repair and new paint. The mechanics of the old tug were adequate, but servicing the engine had fallen behind schedule. Snook found himself feeling relieved that the cost of rejuvenation would fall upon his former first mate and not upon himself. He knew it would be an expensive renovation.

Jared, on the other hand, relished his new role as the captain and owner of the *Rig*. He was anxious for Ponch and Snook to join him and was ready to engage in their *Solstice* recovery plot in exchange for construction work to improve the condition of the *Rig*.

When the ship was tied to the dock, he commanded his less than enthusiastic crew to swab the decks and clean the rooms. Knowing Snook and Ponch would soon arrive, he wanted his vessel to appear "shipshape" and as uncluttered as possible.

After working Baxter and the crew to near exhaustion, Long allowed them to pause when the sound of fluttering, coughing and clanking was heard overhead. Looking up, he yelled to the others,

"Look lively, mates! It's ol' *Sweet Cheeks* herself! Cap'ting Snook will be onboard in five minutes, along with the *Brotherhood's* Benevolent Master. Quick. Put away the swabbing gear and clean yourselves up. All hands on deck in five minutes; looking sharp and standing at attention! It's show time!"

After circling once overhead, Ponch gracefully landed his amphibious relic in the water and taxied slowly to the seaplane dock. Snook opened the passenger door as they neared the pier and stepped out onto the plane's port side pontoon. When the dock was a couple feet away, he stuck out his left leg to slow the plane's momentum and gently eased the craft to the dock. Then he hopped across to the wooden walkway and pulled the tether rope until the plane was close enough to tie it to the buttress.

Once the seaplane was secure, both pilot and passenger quickly walked the wharf planks toward the *Rig* and were onboard in a matter of minutes.

Snook was pleased with the condition of the *Rig* and the uniform sharpness of his former crew. When they stood at attention awaiting inspection, Jared pleased his former boss by declaring "ready for inspection, sir!" He followed his statement with a sharp salute.

With a nod in Jared's direction, Ponch indicated he was impressed. The new owner had humbly acquiesced to reestablish his long friendship with Snook. It was a wise and thoughtful gesture and the Cap'ting felt the vitality of his confidence returning.

"Stand at ease, men!" Long commanded. "This here is Ponch Marchbanks, for those of you who don't know him. He's a good friend and, hopefully, our business associate as well. We have some plans to put into motion this week and I'm gonna' need each of you to step up and do your best work so we can succeed! Cap'ting Snook will fill you in on the scheme."

Snook proceeded to tell the crew about how the *Solstice* had been stolen by some "no good sport fishers." He planted the seed and reconfirmed in everyone's mind that sport fishermen were no good and they were ruining the Alaskan fisheries by pulling out too many fish.

"Fer a long time, fishin' fer sport iz the reason life has bin hard fer us Alaska commercial fishermen." He went on to tell them about how two men in particular had conspired and cheated at *Faro* to steal away the title of the *Solstice*. Snook closed his comments by reminding them that the stolen boat was not even his, but was being leased from Ponch. Yet the "sport fishers" stole it from him anyway.

"They knew it wuzun't mine, but tricked me into signin' a paper... an' then they threw me over th' side and took the boat, lock, stock 'n barrel!"

In an animated discourse and without holding back his mastery of colorful language, Snook instructed the crew as to how they were going to get the *Solstice* back. He also described how they could enjoy some fun and revenge at the expense of the thieves from the lower forty eight. "It's a sur-fire plan!" he concluded.

As the Benevolent Master of the *Brotherhood*, Ponch promised the crew they would be awarded membership into the exclusive fraternity. All that was required for their initiatory prerequisite, would be for them to swear in blood that they would pledge their hearts and souls to recover the possession and ownership of the *Solstice*. "I'm just askin' you to help return the boat to its proper owner," he concluded.

Jared, Dan and the crew of the *Rig* enthusiastically swore allegiance and commitment to the scheme. As was additionally required, they also swore allegiance and commitment to Marchbanks and Snook.

The Russians knew that becoming card carrying members of the *Brotherhood*, even if they were to be no more than mere 'bit actors,' would change the course and quality of their miserable, deck swabbing lives. Belonging to such an elite (albeit clandestine) fraternity was the fastest and surest way to escape their hopeless existence as galley slaves, living in the dungeon squalor of the old and dangerously worn out commercial fishing boat.

Obtaining the secret society's signs, symbols and handshakes was a guaranteed ticket for both to become free men with futures filled with hope, wealth and status!

Yosif Kulavik and Boris Konovalov stared at each other in amazement, knowing they now had prospects of a happy future in America. They were committed to do whatever was necessary to help their bosses succeed.

"Vse, chto nuzhno, Boris!" Yosif smiled. *"Vse, Chto nuzhno!"**

*"Whatever it takes, Boris!" Yosif smiled. "Whatever it takes!"

CHAPTER ELEVEN

SKAFLESTAD & SONS

Randazzle returned his recently adopted Japanese tourists back to the Icy Strait Pointe Cannery, the docking location for their soon to depart cruise ship. His discomfort was gaining momentum, since he was at a loss as to what to tell Skaflestad about the bear attack damage to the van. Keith's return from his Auke Bay helicopter flight with Andy Torgensen was overdue.

In the few short hours that he was trusted to take care of the T.E.C.K.K.* tourist van, not only had the seats and dash been torn to shreds by the conspiring band of city dump bears, but the carpets had also been laid to waste with an excessive splattering of bear scat.

Following the excitement of having had a close encounter with *"yasei no, moretsuna kuma," ("wild, ferocious bears,")* the animated Orientals had not cleaned the bear scat off the bottom of their shoes or treated the smelly stains on the seat of their pants. When they exited the van, their only concern was to rehash their moments of exhilaration. The D.D.S., however, was growing increasingly worried.

"Would you mind giving me some help with a problem I'm having," he asked an attractive, dark haired lady who was walking past the van toward her own parked car. "I'm not from around here and I have an emergency!"

Sue Tyler was born and raised in Georgia, but had lived in Alaska most of her married life. She exuded genuine southern hospitality and her southern accent gave her away as a non-Alaskan native.

"Aahd be happy to help y'all," she drawled. "Oh, my goodness. What is that terrible odor? Keith really needs to do a little house cleaning in that van of his!"

"That's the problem and I need your help," Randazzle explained. "Bears got inside the tourist van, and you can see and smell the outcome! Where can I get this thing cleaned up before he comes back from Nugget Falls?"

"Ha! Just another day in Bearadise!" she smiled. "Follow me to my place. With a little elbow grease, we can get it cleaned up in no time at all!"

"Thanks," Randazzle smiled in relief. "Keith was helping me out and I'm afraid I let him down."

As they were passing the city dock, Sue spotted Keith's sons, Killian, Kole and Torsten and waived Randazzle to the side of the road. "Pull down to the dock," she instructed. "I want you to meet the Skaflestad boys."

When the young men noticed the familiar van pulling down the boardwalk driveway, they stopped work and came out onto the pier. Their smiles turned inquisitive when they saw the unfamiliar driver behind the wheel. All three walked to the van and were introduced by Sue to the driver.

"Whew! What's that horrible smell?" Killian asked. "And what the heck happened in the van?"

100

Randazzle started to explain. Seeing his discomfort, all three Skaflestads broke out in broad smiles as the adventure unfolded. "I'll bet the orientals were scared out of their wits!" Torsten laughed.

"Not really," Randazzle explained. "They thought it was the most exciting adventure of their lives! I speak a little Japanese, but they were talking so fast, I couldn't keep up with what they were saying. I could tell by the way they responded, though, that it was an exciting adventure for them!"

"Well, even with the damage, it's all good," Kole laughed. "They'll tell their friends and we'll have so much business we won't be able to keep up with it. We'll have to get a second van just to accommodate everyone. Going to the dump needs to become a regular part of the tour. Dad doesn't really take guests there, he just suggests it as a joke!"

Killian took charge, "Torsten, you and Kole go pull the crab cages without me. I'll take the van and get it fixed up as best I can." He instructed Randazzle to join his brothers. The threesome left the van and boarded the *Karen Marie* to finish their crab catching preparations. Killian drove Sue back to her parked car at the top of the city dock driveway and then took the van to the T.E.C.K.K. warehouse for cleaning and repair, hoping to find a roll of duct tape to mask the damage.

"Soon," he thought, "the torn seats and dash board will be patched and the duct tape will add one more hair raising story to our action-packed T.E.C.K.K. Outfitters bear hunt adventure."

After scrubbing out the bear scat and liberally spraying pine scent to alleviate the lingering stench, Killian added his personal touch to the reconditioned van. He draped a recently tanned brown bear hide over the damaged back seat. The young Tlingit had a flair for what cruise ship tourists might want to see on their guided bear hunt. From that time forward,

T.E.C.K.K. guests would feel an even closer affinity to the Alaskan wild.

Torsten and Kole took Randazzle to their favorite crabbing location at Fingers Bay, a few miles west of the Hoonah harbor. The Skaflestad boys had prepared an adequate supply of salmon heads to bait the cages. As in the past, their plan was to pull up their cages and harvest the catch. After harvesting, they would fill the cages with new bait and send them back down to the bottom again. It was an exercise that was profitable, but with different degrees of success in each cage.

Randazzle felt privileged to have the opportunity to be a participant on the family's crabbing run. He enthusiastically joined in the work as his new friends pulled up cage after cage and extracted the Dungeness crab into the *Karen Marie's* holding tank. After an hour of activity, most of the cages were emptied. They were then re-baited with salmon heads and entrails. The trio paused in mid action when they heard the noisy, hovering sound of a helicopter overhead. It was Keith returning from his covert day trip to Nuggett Falls with Officer Torgensen.

Andy steadily hovered his copter twenty feet above the *Karen Marie* while Keith, hand over hand, shimmied down a thick, dangling rope that was lowered from the helicopter door. Within seconds, he landed squarely in the open area toward the back of the boat. After he released the rope, the helicopter veered eastward and up and Andy was gone as quickly as he had appeared. After a brief period of time, a well-equipped commercial fishing boat named the *Janice K* eased gently along the port side of the *Karen Marie*.

"Grampa!" exclaimed Torsten. "What're you doing here?"

Faggan Skaflestad, Keith's father and the boys' grandfather, was a surprisingly small and wiry man. He was dark from his long and constant fishing days in the outdoors, coupled with his Tlingit and Norwegian mixed lineage.

"When he was leaving Nuggett Falls, your dad called and told me you were out here crabbing. He asked me to meet here to take you home. He'll finish the crabbing," Faggan responded over the noise of the sea. "Hop aboard, boys!"

The brothers did as told and after hauling the barrels filled with crab from the *Karen Marie* to the *Janice K*, they left the calm waters of Fingers Bay and headed toward Hoonah with their grandfather.

Keith busied himself by rolling up the last of the ropes and putting away the remaining crabbing equipment on board. He then directed Randazzle to go inside the cabin and prepare to go to Glacier Bay. "Afterward," Keith promised, "you'll get to join your group at the lodge over at Excursion."

Even though he enjoyed himself in Hoonah and as a helper on the crabbing boat, the D.D.S. was relieved to realize he would soon be headed toward his fishing lodge destination. Although he had fallen a day behind the others, he was enthused to get back on track with his planned fishing trip.

"What do you have going on at Glacier Bay," Randazzle innocently asked Keith.

"Just checking in with some old adversaries," he replied. "I heard they're busy refurbishing a commercial fishing boat and I want to stop by and take a look. Besides, for a peace offering, I'll take them a few fresh crabs for dinner!"

"Sounds like a plan," was the reply. "I'm getting hungry myself, so I hope you've kept out enough crab for all of us to eat!"

On their way across the Icy Strait, Randazzle disclosed the damage the tourist van had encountered. Keith laughed and replied "I already know all about it! I got the word from Sue and then later from Killian. Don't worry, we turn lemons into lemonade around here. Can you imagine how excited tourists will be when they get to be in a van that was vandalized by bears? T.E.C.K.K. Outfitters will be famous! Thanks for going out to the dump to let those bears ravage my van!"

Keith was sincere and Randazzle was relieved. He had not looked at it from Skaflestad's tourism point of view and he felt good about the tour guide's attitude and response.

Twenty minutes after leaving Fingers, they entered the protected waters of Glacier Bay. Captain Skaflestad connected with the park service and received verbal authorization to enter the park as well as permission to tether the *Karen Marie* at the dock adjacent to the *Glacier Bay Lodge*.

"Let's go have some fun," Keith instructed Randazzle after he grabbed the bucket holding the live crabs. Both men disembarked and worked together to tie down the boat. Then, in haste, they walked down the long wooden pier toward the partially hidden *Rig*.

---

*The initials T.E.C.K.K. stand for Keith Skaflestad's family: Torsten (youngest son), Edna (wife), Clarence (Keith's first given name), Killian (oldest son) and Kolbjorn "Kole" (middle son).

CHAPTER TWELVE

ARCTIC BROTHERHOOD

Since 1899, a fraternal organization known as the *Arctic Brotherhood* has existed in the Pacific Northwest. From the turn of the last century, chapters have dotted the Alaskan landscape from the original *Camp No. 1* in Skagway to settlements deep within the Klondike gold fields.

As reported by Ken Spotwood of the *Klondike Sun*, "It wasn't long before every northern frontier town and settlement of any importance boasted its own *Arctic Brotherhood* chapter. Eventually, thirty two camps were established. At its height, the Arctic Brotherhood boasted some ten thousand members.

"The preamble of its constitution stated: 'The object of this organization shall be to encourage and promote social and intellectual intercourse and benevolence among its neighbors, and to advance the interests of its members, and those of the Northwest section of North America.

"*Camp No. 1* of the Arctic Brotherhood was established in Skagway, Alaska, in 1899 following the arrival of the Ocean

Steamer *City of Seattle*. The membership roster, boasting eleven members, soon swelled to more than three hundred, as the roots of the *Arctic Brotherhood* spread among the miners readying themselves for the trip up and over Chilcoot pass en route to the Klondike gold fields.

"Historian I. N. Davidson reports 'There were the usual objections to secret orders made to this new order by the churches, and the term "Arctic Bummers" on one side and "Sniveling Hypocrites" on the other were frequently heard.'

"The skeptics were silenced when they saw that the lodge looked after its members in sickness and health, buried its dead and generally improved educational and social conditions of the booming mining camps.

"It wasn't long before every northern city, town or settlement of any importance boasted its *Arctic Brotherhood* camp. Over the next century, the usefulness and need for the *Arctic Brotherhood* waned and its membership greatly diminished. Civilization brought in churches and other competing benevolent organizations. As the ranks of wildcat gold miners declined, the need for the *Arctic Brotherhood* seemed to wane."

Observers might have assumed the membership disappeared altogether; but insiders know that is not the case. At least one renegade faction has long since separated from the main body and promulgated on its own. Focused on developing talent in the performing arts in and around the Icy Strait, the *Arctic Brotherhood* schism transformed into a tightly knit fraternity with its mantle of authority resting on the broad shoulders of Glacier Bay's Ponch Marchbanks. Eschewing up line authority, this rogue chapter evolved and took on the nickname of the *Icy Brotherhood*. In time, the moniker was shortened and the group was known throughout southeast Alaska simply as the *Brotherhood*.

The uncontested Benevolent Master's network of loyal accomplices consisted of an eclectic band of fishermen and seafaring merchants whose activities were centered in and around the Icy Strait. The *Brotherhood* not only protected the safety of its membership, but also became a troupe committed to the goal of improving the financial well-being of its hearty "band of brothers."

Fraternal meeting times and locations became a movable feast. Secret signs and handshakes were employed to identify those who belonged to the *Brotherhood* from those who did not. The guarded salutations were also used to differentiate a member's personal level of talent and authority.

What began as a training guild in early Icy Strait society, developed over decades into a clandestine catalyst that staged suspenseful dramas and intriguing plays. Eventually, there were very few locals who chose to escape involvement in the society's ongoing productions.

Even though members were often at odds with one another, their motto was to do "whatever it takes" to perform their organized theatrics and bring their orchestrated monkey business to fruition.

The rewards for participants were commensurate with the individual risks that were taken. Ultimately, the association entrenched itself as a noteworthy force throughout the majestic waterways of the fabled Inside Passage. Cruise ship tourists and unsuspecting sport fishermen were not given immunity and often, albeit innocently, found themselves at the center of the fraternity's productions.

There has not been another group in the vicinity of the Icy Strait that has generated more stories of skullduggery and shenanigans than those that have been created by the *Brotherhood*.

CHAPTER THIRTEEN

GAMES OF CHANCE

Several hours prior to the arrival of the *Karen Marie*, Jared was lying on his back drilling a small hole under one of the tables in what was becoming the *Rig's* new casino. Upon completion, he removed himself to the newly refurbished stateroom opposite the casino, where he bore another small hole beneath the lower bunk bed.

Long then fixed a nail into a spring and fastened the spring on the underside of the floor, so that the nail could come up through the floor under the table. Next, he attached a halibut fishing line (eighty pound test) to the spring and ran it up the wall and into the stateroom. He then drilled a third hole, this time in the bulkhead of the stateroom, just above the top berth. From that position, an agile person such as himself could comfortably lie down in the berth and look out into the cabin.

When gaming began, it was their plan to seat Ponch at the poker table in a chair located on the starboard side of the stateroom. The gambler's chair opposite the dealer (in the third base position) was perfectly situated to successfully carry out their gambling scheme. Nothing was left to chance.

The strategy involved having Long lie down out of sight in the upper berth while the game was in progress. His job was to look through the peep-hole and if the "mark" had one pair he would pull the fishing line once; if two pair, twice; if threes, three times; and if fours, four times. If the competition held a straight or flush, he was to frantically flutter the nail. Prior to beginning the card games, Ponch was instructed to kick off one boot, as if to relax, and put his bare foot over the nail. Through this means, he could easily be made aware of what hand the opposition held.

After the carpentry was completed, Ponch decided to strengthen his Texas Hold 'em card playing ability. To further perfect his skills of deception, the crew members (excepting Long and McGee) were not made aware of the peep-hole and fishing line that had been put in place to insure Ponch's advantage.

Desiring an opportunity to test their scheme, Yosif and Boris were invited to rest from their carpentry labors and join them in a game of cards. Eager to ply their gambling skills against the house, the Russians readily accepted. Unwittingly, they ran to their quarters and returned with a small leather pouch that represented their meager joint life savings.

When everyone was seated at their respective locations, Jared looked through the peep-hole and gave Ponch the prearranged signal, letting him know that he was set to go. To begin the game, however, took longer than anticipated. The Russian fishermen had to be taught the fundamental rules of *Texas Hold 'em*.

In the darkness of the ship's galley, they had gambled nightly with fellow crew members. However, because of their heritage, neither had ever heard of the game *Texas Hold 'em*. After considerable instructions, they eventually declared that they understood the rules well enough to start the game.

Before the cards were dealt, Ponch made a public display of taking off his left boot, "just to relax." To his dread, however, nothing happened. He wiggled the nail with his big toe, but there was still no response. What the old bush pilot did not realize was that during the instruction period, Jared had fallen asleep.

The owner of the *Rig* had worked a long shift, sailing from Lisianski Inlet to Glacier Bay. He then endured another long stretch while working to get the *Rig* in shipshape condition. Finally, he fought off his tiredness and spent many more hours doing the carpentry work to refurbish the *Rig*. These shifts were all worked in succession and without any rest in between.

The extensive gambling instructions that were given to the crew while he was resting on the upper bunk in the stateroom, combined with the slow side-to-side rolling motion of the boat, was just too much of a challenge for him to overcome. He had simply dozed off.

Ponch quickly lost three hands and a considerable amount of money while he was waiting for Long's signals. The Russian crew members were excited and increasingly animated with their gambling success. Ponch, however, could wait no longer. The Master picked up a spittoon and let it fly in the direction of the stateroom wall. Immediately thereafter, communications were restored and he received his signals promptly.

After the unexplained change of luck and once his winnings and his seed money were lost, Yosif ventured to ask Ponch why he threw the spittoon. Ponch told him that when the cards were running so badly against him, he remembered what an old gambler once told him: that it was a good change of luck to kick over a spittoon. "In the heat of the moment," he explained, "I thought I would not only kick it over, but that I would break the damned thing all to pieces."

Stoically listening to his reply, Boris replied, "Ya. I saw that yer luck changed right after y' threw the spittoon. I'll try it m'self, next time I've a run a' bad luck."

During a lull in the gambling, they heard a shout from the pier: *"Permission to come aboard!"* It was Skaflestad and Randazzle wanting to board the boat. Two new men translated into fresh gambling money, so Ponch invited them aboard. Fate had delivered new "marks" at just the right time.

With their pockets emptied, Yosif and Boris were excused to go back to their carpentry work. Randazzle and Skaflestad were pleasantly surprised when they were invited to sit in the chairs so recently vacated by the Russians. With slaps on their backs, they were encouraged to "belly up" for a friendly wager and a little *Chardonneal* from the *Rig's* wine cellar.

Randazzle asked Skaflestad to lend him two hundred dollars for gambling money and the amiable Hoonah tour guide happily obliged. Soon, they were engaged in the heat of the game. This time, however, Jared did not doze off and the visitors were methodically relieved of their money.

Ponch, Jared and Snook knew they had designed an efficient and effective gambling machine and they were increasingly confident that the *Solstice* would soon be back into the hands of her rightful owner.

As mentioned, it only took a few hands of *Texas Hold 'em* to empty the visitor's pockets. More correctly, Skaflestad's pockets were emptied and Randazzle was deeply in debt from borrowing from Skaflestad. Neither suspected the cause of their serial losses and both had given up hope of recovery. They left the *Rig* with their tails between their legs, vowing to return when Lady Luck was once again on their side. The crab bucket and crabs that were initially brought as gifts were the last items the pair lost at the poker table.

Buoyed by their aberrant gambling success, the captain and crew of the *Rig* celebrated by melting down half a bucket of butter. They then steamed and devoured their clam bounty. When they had washed the feast down with their private label of vineyard grog, they rested for a time and then commenced to inspect their newly rehabilitated sea vessel.

Using cast off material from the *Glacier Bay Lodge*, the boats interior had been refitted to suit the taste of the most demanding gentleman. The sitting rooms were plush and comfortable with the woodwork sanded and stained to a degree that rivaled the finest quality. The casino was reminiscent of an English pub and included a "Puff and Dart" wall in one corner. The Tewkesbury inspired bar was lavish, thanks to Jared's woodworking talent and his commitment to detail. The interior of the *Rig* had been resurrected.

Untying from the dock the next morning took very little time for the enthusiastic crew. The *Rig* left Bartlett Cove and traveled north by northwest, weaving her way through the Beardslee Islands. This out of the way course was followed to give the new owner an opportunity to fully acquaint himself with captaining the ship.

After running a full set of maneuvers, Captain Long opted for a show of camaraderie and he turned the sailing of the ship over to Snook. "You've sailed the ol' boat more than me," he confided, "and I don't want anything to happen to her now that she's been rebuilt!"

After Long cleared the islands, Snook took over and redirected the ship one hundred sixty degrees toward due south. Following that course, it was only a short time before the seamen exited the protected waters of Glacier Bay and entered the Icy Strait. Sighting Lemesurier Island on his right, Snook turned sharply to the left and pointed the *Rig* easterly toward Excursion Inlet. After viewing the Gustavus pier in his eyeglass, he corrected thirty degrees southeast and traveled on the south side of Pleasant Island. Once past Pleasant, the Porpoise Islands were in view. Following his GPS, he commandeered his vessel between the southeast corner of Pleasant Island and the northernmost Porpoise Island.

When Excursion Inlet was in sight, the *Rig* gradually slowed to ten knots. Snook then carefully drifted to a stop above a GPS point identified as the Russian Hump.

The Russian Hump has long been a favorite spot for halibut fishermen. It is located about five hundred feet offshore from the southwest entrance to Excursion Inlet. Not coincidentally, the Russian Hump is directly across from, and in full view of the *Alaskan Bear Lodge*. With binoculars, the conspirators could see every activity occurring across the channel on the southeastern shore entrance to Excursion Inlet.

They prepared to anchor at a location Ponch and Snook had determined to be an ideal staging location for their nefarious high seas scheme. Ponch was lock-jaw determined to get the *Solstice* back and Snook was hell bent on getting revenge on the two actors who had thrown him into the icy waters near Vanderbilt Reef.

When the anchor was dropped, all activities that followed presented the outward appearance that the *Rig* was just another boat that had stopped to fish for halibut. To complete the illusion, hooks were baited and lines were dropped to the bottom of the sea.

While dropping the lines, Ponch spewed his frustration above the sound of the wind and the waves in the direction of the lodge: *"You damned boat thieves'll be brought to justice in twenty four hours, or we'll all be buried at sea together!"*

There was no mistaking the Benevolent Master's pent up anger directed toward two of the lodge's fishing guests. To make matters worse, the *Solstice* was docked at the pier across the inlet in clear view of the occupants of the *Rig*. According to Ponch's oath, she would soon be returned to her rightful owner, regardless of loss of life or limb. The thieving card sharks that had stolen her from Snook were targeted to pay for their crime.

After details were squared away, Jared boarded the *Fish 'n Chips*, a twelve foot aluminum skiff that was kept on the deck of the *Rig*. He paddled quietly across the inlet, heavily armed with professionally designed flyers.

On paper similar to parchment and penned in old style font and format, the announcement read as follows:

ALL FISHERMEN ARE INVITED TO JOIN IN AN EVENING OF GAMING, DRINKING & ENTERTAINMENT ABOARD THE RIG.

FESTIVITIES WILL COMMENCE AT 1900 HOURS.

THIS EVENT IS SPONSORED BY THE BROTHERHOOD,

A FRATERNAL ORGANIZATION WHOSE OBJECTIVE
IS TO ENCOURAGE & PROMOTE SOCIAL & INTELLECTUAL
INTERCOURSE & BENEVOLENCE AMONGST
MEMBERS & FRIENDS.

The trap had been set. Having been given several handbills, lodge keeper McMichaels made sure each of his guests were given a copy. To a man, they swallowed the bait: hook, line and sinker.

• • •

When McMichaels and his lodgers boarded the *Rig* that evening, it was already crowded with fishermen-turned-gamblers, including the return of former victims: Skaflestad and Randazzle. The casino was buzzing with the excitement of gambling activity.

Ponch's table was engaged in a lively game of *Three Card Monte* when Keith surprised the host by making an approach to his table. Out of the blue, he began telling the others not to bet because "the game was rigged."

Keith had taken it as his duty to warn the others of underhanded gambling and he commenced to try to stop them with a push and a punch to the arm; but finally, he outright told everyone not to bet. Skaflestad passed the word to everyone that would listen that Ponch was a professional gambler and would take their money, often at the moment when they mistakenly thought the game was turning in their favor.

Despite becoming annoyed, Ponch put up with Keith's interference and behavior for some time. Eventually though, he put his cards down in frustration and invited everyone to join him in a drink. When the liquor was flowing freely, he excused himself from the crowd, announcing "I'm suffering with a toothache and need to go to my room."

When he returned to the casino, it had gotten chilly, so he took a seat near the stove. Several of the men joined him, seating themselves around the stove in a half circle. As men always do, they started telling one another their favorite fishing stories. Ponch's tooth apparently continued to ache so badly, however, that he apologized and said he could not enjoy their company any longer because of the pain.

Many remedies for the toothache were volunteered, but in most cases, the necessary ingredients were not available on the boat. Finally, Johnny Crabill, who had become the *Rig's* barkeeper, recommended to Ponch that he should hold hot seasoning on the side of his face. Ponch asked Johnny if he had any seasoning and Crabill promptly retrieved a plastic container from the pantry labeled *Johnny's Seasoning*.

Crabill then poured a liberal amount of the seasoning into a napkin. He twisted the ends of the paper together to keep the salt-like seasoning from spilling. When finished, it looked like a ball about the size of an egg. He then put the napkin in a small leather pouch to prevent it from combusting when placed on the stove. After it got sufficiently hot, he took the napkin and seasoning out of the pouch and held it on Ponch's face, next to his sore tooth. When the paper cooled, it was returned the pouch and put back on the stove to reheat.

When the process had been repeated a few times, Ponch excused himself and went to his room to get a wet wash cloth. While he was absent, the barkeeper shouted to the crowd, "In the festive spirit of the evening, let's have some fun with Marchbanks." He then opened the small paper bundle, dumped out the seasoning and, for everyone to see, refilled it with pepper from a shaker.

When Ponch returned, he picked up the package and again held it to his face. Sitting nearby, Jared asked him if the seasoning was doing his tooth any good and Ponch replied that he thought it was. Some of the fishermen laughed at him for thinking that hot seasoning could help a toothache, so Crabill stepped up and said "Marchbanks, do you know that when seasoning gets hot it turns into pepper?"

"No, I didn't know that," Ponch replied. "What do you take me for, anyway, an idiot? You must have had too much to drink tonight."

With everyone in on the joke except Ponch, the crowd laughed and Crabill spoke up again, saying "I don't believe you have any seasoning left inside that paper."

Ponch set the package back on the stove and replied "You must take me for a damned fool, Johnny and I'm convinced you haven't any common sense at all. I got the seasoning right out of your container and I tasted it before I wrapped it up. I know its seasoning salt and that settles it!"

"But Ponch," Johnny argued, "don't you know that seasoning turns to pepper when it gets hot? I'll bet drinks for everyone that there's no seasoning left inside that paper on the stove. That bag is full of pepper!"

The crowd laughed once again at Ponch's expense. This time, however, he got mad, jumped up on his chair and waved his arms. "John! I'll bet you five hundred dollars that there's nothing in that paper but seasoning!"

With the same enthusiasm, Crabill stepped up and shouted "I'll take that bet!"

Ponch pulled a wad of cash from his pocket and counted out five hundred in small bills. Crabill pulled out his money clip and started counting, but he could only come up with three fifty.

In an indignant tone, Ponch, declared that he would not bet for less than five hundred and he informed the bartender that he would let him back out of the bet. Johnny then pulled out a vial filled with small gold nuggets and declared that it was worth much more than five hundred and he would bet that instead of the cash. Ponch promptly accepted the wager.

Just as they were about to reveal the contents inside the paper, Ponch turned to the crowd and said, "Does anyone else want to get in on this? You high rollers were laughing at me a minute ago! Now, put up or shut up!"

From the back of the room, Kulavik yelled out "They switched 'da bag on ya, Ponch! Don't lose yar money. It's a fool's bet!" The warning was to no avail. Everyone could see that Ponch was mad and he could not be convinced that a switch had taken place.

Devin stepped forward and declared that he would bet one hundred dollars.

"Nothing less than five hundred!" Ponch countered. "Are you a man or not? You have to bet five hundred to even be in this wager!"

In confidence, Crabill said to Dev, "Ponch is just trying to bluff you out of the bet, but he can't bluff me. I'm gonna take his money!"

With such encouragement, Devin grew confident and he worked the crowd until he had borrowed four hundred dollars from two of his lodge guests. When it was in hand, he slapped the money on the bar and Crabill promptly scooped it into a large leather pouch that also contained his own gold nuggets and the rest of the gambling money. True to his word, Ponch matched Devin's bet with another five hundred dollars, taken from his wad of small bills.

Next, Liddiard took the lead for the fishermen and gambled a thousand dollars. Several others were enticed and also became invested. When wagering closed, the pot had grown to over ten thousand dollars.

Excitement in the casino increased when the paper bag was taken off the stove and handed to the bartender. He slowly untwisted the paper and spread it out on the counter. To the amazement of all, the contents were revealed to be as nice and fine of a pile of *Johnny's Seasoning* as could be imagined.

For a final effect, Ponch licked his finger and touched it to the seasoning. "It's still as tasty as Johnny's Seasoning can be and there's no pepper in there at all!" he exclaimed. "Now, give me my money!"

The barkeeper handed a smiling Ponch the leather pouch.

"Never mess with the *Brotherhood*!" the Master shouted to the disgruntled horde of gamblers. If any of them had been paying attention, they would have noticed that his toothache had somehow magically disappeared.

When Gary took a large pinch of the seasoning to taste it for himself, it almost strangled him. However, the gagging might have been caused by the loss of his thousand dollars. For some time afterward, every time someone at the lodge asked him to pass the *Johnny's Seasoning*, he would get sick all over again.

Later in the week when retelling the story with the sport fishermen out of earshot, Ponch recounted to a smiling *Brotherhood* audience that they had "caught suckers before, but these were the first ones that he and Johnny had ever seasoned!"

...

After the excitement from the toothache episode had subsided, gambling got back to normal and soon the chairs at every gaming spot in the casino were full. Patrons who could not secure a seat loitered around those who had, looking wistfully over their shoulder while watching for their own chance at the table.

The background noise in the *Rig's* casino was deafening. A flamboyant entertainer dressed in Mississippi riverboat attire banged out ragtime music on the upright piano in the corner of the room. Suds flowed freely and were served in frosted glass mugs adorned with the *Rig's* personalized logo.

Fishermen turned gamblers shouted and jeered at one another as they won or lost stacks of cash, jewelry, fishing lures, poker chips and whatever else they had on hand to wager at the gaming tables.

A pair of blonde, long legged, look alike bar waitresses with "Yvonne" and "Yvette" etched on their respective name tags, nonchalantly sashayed from table to table serving drinks. Scantily clad in dangerously short casino outfits, neither seemed to mind that they were flirting with men who, for the most part, possessed countenances that could scare the liquor right out of a glass of whiskey.

Technically, the *Rig* was at sea, and in those remote climes, testosterone raged. The perfumed hour glass figures with lace covered limbs piqued the prurient instincts of the purest of the gamblers. Men who knew better transformed into stereotypical males with the accompanying attention deficit arousal.

The beautiful ladies were hired to do everything and anything they could dream up to loosen the inhibitions of the gamblers. They passed out free cigars and martinis and bashfully winked whenever eye contact was made. The men at the tables lost concentration and when they lost money, they did not feel that they had been taken advantage of in the slightest. The cast and their audience were happy and as festivities progressed, they were getting happier!

The *Rig's* gaming room increasingly became a sweatbox packed with fishermen. The casino was filled with colorful, loud language and stifling cigar smoke. As the evening wore on, the men aboard became transubstantiated gamblers, reveling in an Alaskan Mardi Gras on Fat Tuesday.

Without advanced warning, a shrill screech blared from the microphone, piercing the air near the piano stage. Following the screech was a loud tap, tap, tapping sound and, as if on cue, the room transformed from noisy gambling mayhem to complete silence.

Ponch Marchbank's deep, rich voice filled the void: "Gentlemen! Your attention! Please join me in a loud Alaskan welcome to tonight's entertainment. Here to perform for us, from Juneau's famous Red Dog Saloon.... please welcome Mr. Phineas Poon!"

Excitement ensued as floodlights darted and ricocheted around the dimly lit, humanity packed honky-tonk. The spotlights finally stopped and focused on the piano, where an impish entertainer burst loudly into an old ragtime version of the *Maple Leaf Rag*. The crowd howled and cheered when he joyfully shouted "Who says ragtime is dead? ...hell, I didn't even know it was sick!"

With masterfully exaggerated animation, Poon made the transition from ragtime to his patented barroom style sing-a-long. In the middle of a lively refrain of *"Comin' Round the Mountain,"* Poon stopped short:

"Hey Grantley. Did I tell you I got a new fly rod and reel for my wife?"

"Why, no, you didn't!" Grantley shot back.

"Yeah, I really did! It was the best trade I've ever made!"

The crowd exploded with laughter and everyone joined in as he resumed *"Comin' Round the Mountain."* Soon, however, there was another pregnant pause:

"Hey, Jared!"

"Yeah, Phineas, what is it?"

"The other day, I read about the evils of drinking... so what could I do?"

"I don't know, Phineas, what did you do?"

"Well, I gave up reading, of course!"

To the hoots and hollers of the men, the singing came back with new energy until there was yet another hesitation:

"Hey, Ponch. There are old pilots and there are bold pilots... but there are NO old bold pilots! You're the exception!" The crowd roared its approval.

"Yeah, Phineas" Ponch replied. "I've always said that any landing you walk away from is a good one!"

"Hey, Skaflestad!" he yelled to the Hoonah native sitting at the gambling table on the far end of the room. What's the difference between a commercial fisherman and Bigfoot?"

"Why, I have no idea, Phineas. What's the difference?"

"Well," explained Poon. "One is covered with matted hair and smells awful. The other has big feet!"

There was back slapping and jeering as Skaflestad, in exaggerated form, smelled his armpits... and then the piano playing and the singing resumed.

"Hey, McMichaels, you damned cheapskate!" Poon shouted at the lodge keeper. "What's the difference between a twelve foot skiff and a fisherman?"

"I'll be danged if I know, Phineas. What's the difference?"

"A twelve foot skiff will sometimes tip, you tightwad!"

...and again the piano played and the men sang even louder than before.

"Johnny! They say a fool and his money are soon parted!"

"Yeah. I've heard that, Phineas," Johnny shot back. "My question to you, though, is how did the fool and his money get together in the first place? I've always said 'a fool and his money are soon partying!' ...so, let's PARTY ON!"

The crowd roared and Phineas went back to pounding on his piano, banging out ragtime tunes louder that anyone thought possible. Poker cards were dealt and drinking and gambling resumed. The gaming room aboard the *Rig* was the place to be that night and a more raucous crowd did not exist in all of the Great Land, or possibly anywhere else on planet Earth.

As the evening progressed, Lady Luck smiled on Dusty and Tyrone. They had been perched for over an hour at the first and third base positions on the *Rig's* blackjack table and their cards had repeatedly turned up winners.

The actors' blackjack hands prevailed over the house time and time again as they split aces, bought insurance and recklessly drew on every hand below 17. On the few occasions when they lost, they doubled down until they were winners once again. The men could do no wrong.

In exasperation, the dealer "Yosif Kulavik from Kamchatka, Russia" (as advertised on his name tag) threw his large and weathered hands skyward in despair. "Enuff! Enuff! Y've broka d' bank! I catcha-hell fruma da boss! Blacka-jacka is now aclosed!"

With the confidence of world champion card sharks, the confident thespian gamblers happily funneled their substantial winnings into their backpacks and exited the newly closed blackjack table.

After wandering the casino, they approached the corner of the room that harbored the poker table. Both smiled when they read "BENEVOLENT MASTER" elegantly engraved in capital letters on a brass placard hanging on the wall above the table. Inexplicably, two chairs were suddenly vacated, comfortably adjacent to the casino's back wall. Seeing their opportunity, Dusty and Tyrone filled the seats, happy with their good timing.

"When you're hot, you're hot!" Dusty shouted to Ty over the crowd noise. Turning toward the dealer wearing a name tag identifying him as PONCH, he shouted "Deal 'em up, amigo... and kiss goodbye to your pesos, hombre!"

The dealer smiled widely at the newcomers now gracing his table. With an exaggerated accent, even though he did not have a drop of Hispanic blood in his veins, he replied, "Bienvenida, Amigos." He then gently kicked the tip of a small nail protruding through the floor beneath his feet and began to deal the cards, slowly and deliberately.

To obtain every possible advantage, Ponch stealthily slipped the Xtra Tuff fishing boot off his left foot and placed his unprotected arch squarely over the nail. He knew Jared was awake and fully engaged as soon as he felt three distinct twitches from the nail. Game on.

Gambling strategy had been discussed by the dealer and his confidence man prior to when the *Rig* had left Glacier Bay and the gamesmen stayed true to their outline. To increase his marks' confidence, Ponch discreetly used Jared's signals to let the two actors win a few hands. Thanks to his accomplice's attentiveness and the thoroughness of their preparation rehearsals, Ponch knew the value of each gambler's hand in advance of betting. The house executed each round of cards with full awareness.

As they continued to win, the nonplused gamblers increased their boldness and became more and more reckless and their wagering increased in aggressiveness. Ponch plied his fisherman skills as he generously laid out more bait, all the while continuing to inflate the gamblers egos.

When he knew the hook was set deep and hard, he moved fast. Each time the house won, he encouraged the gamblers to double down and even triple down "to get their money back." It was not long before the old Master had taken back all of their evening's winnings and after a few additional hands, he worked on becoming the owner of everything of value that they had brought on board with them.

The stakes went higher and higher and the attention of everyone in the room gravitated toward the poker table. All watched and witnessed Ponch's final triumphant dagger when, under extreme emotional duress to the actors, he reclaimed the signed and witnessed title to the *Solstice*.

At the moment the title to the commercial fishing catamaran changed hands, a familiar stench filled their nostrils. It was a smell even stronger than the cigar smoke and fisherman sweat that permeated the casino. In unison, they shuddered when they heard an eerily familiar, high pitched laugh emanating from the foul smell that was just inches from the back of their heads.

"Now, hows 'bout wagerin' some a' yer movie royalties, ya' damned scumbags!"

The alcoholic stench combined with waves of horrid breath passing through rotted teeth was memorable. The rancid, urine smelling clothing and neglected personal hygiene was unmistakable.

Dusty and Tyrone knew they were once again in the presence of their nemesis, Cap'ting Snook McGee.

CHAPTER FOURTEEN

TRIAL AND ERROR

In the midst of Snook's polluted atmosphere, Dusty and Tyrone knew they were in trouble. After a quick glance into the stern face of the poker dealer, then catching the sober expression of the bartender, and finally, after searching the faces of the other locals in the room, they concluded it was worse. "Being in trouble" was ratcheted up to "being in danger." It became obvious to them that the floating casino was a prop for a well-orchestrated gambling sting and their swift change of luck was a conspiracy that was cunningly engineered by their hosts. They both knew they had been targeted and duped.

After making brief eye contact with one another, the duo turned and with lightening precision, began to pummel the scraggy, unkempt face of Cap'ting Snook. As their arch enemy's blood and snot splattered against the galley wall, they soon realized the repulsive fisherman had a host of friends on board.

Fraternal shouts from one member of the *Brotherhood* to another rang loudly above the increasing madness that dominated the ship's casino. Secret hand signs were flashed and unknown code words and phrases were signaled.

Standing back-to-back, a fighting stance they quickly assumed in their desperate effort to fend off all comers, Dusty and Tyrone did not have time to assess the impending crush of Alaskan fishermen that encircled and brought them both into submission. Within minutes, the angry entourage beat them both to a bloody, unconscious pulp. The actors' excruciating pain from multiple injuries was mercifully masked by their imminent unconsciousness.

When they were revived with smelling salts, to their joint consternation, both were in ankle and wrist shackles and were seated in chairs that appeared to be arranged for them as defendants in a maritime court of law. The casino had hastily been refashioned to resemble a courtroom. They were prisoners in a hostile tribunal.

Seated next to them was their fishing companion, Gary Liddiard, who had volunteered to act as their trial attorney. "I once intended to become an attorney," he confidently admitted to the defendants, "before the opportunity to become a Hollywood make-up artist came my way. From the movies and television shows I've watched, I think I've developed the demeanor and presence of mind to represent you well. I'm sure we can get the charges against you dismissed."

"Charges? What charges?" asked Dusty. "We haven't done anything wrong!"

"I've been handed this paper outlining why you were arrested," Gary answered as he waved an official looking document in the air. "It says your 'charges include, but are not limited to, disorderly conduct, public intoxication, inciting a riot, cheating at games of chance and stealing a commercial fishing boat.' It doesn't look good, but at least they're providing you your day in court!"

"Jeeze," Ty managed. "We just came here to fish. Can they really do this to us?"

"All rise," newly appointed bailiff, Johnny Crabill, enunciated in a strong and loud voice as a man dressed in judicial robes entered the room. "All rise for the honorable Judge Poncherello Marchbanks, Benevolent Master of the *Brotherhood*. It is he who is charged with dispensing justice on the high seas in and around the Icy Strait."

A colorful parrot perched on the judge's right shoulder, cocked his head sharply to listen while His Honor paused and looked around the room prior to speaking.

"Please be seated," Marchbanks finally instructed as he gathered his flowing judicial robes tightly around his waist and sat down.

When all were settled and the noise had subsided, he announced in an authoritative voice, "We are assembled here to render legal judgment at the joint trial of Dusty O'Neal and Tyrone "T-Bone" Jameson. Will the two defendants and their illustrious attorney please stand so all may get a good look at you?"

All three of the men stood up. The chains and shackles restricting Dusty and Tyrone were awkward and heavy and they created a great deal of noise each time the defendants moved.

"Please note in the record," said the judge, "that these defendants have been accused, arrested and are on trial for charges of disorderly conduct, public intoxication, inciting a riot, cheating at games of chance and also, for stealing a valuable commercial fishing boat. How do you plead?"

"Not guilty on all counts," replied Liddiard forcefully.

"We will see," smirked the judge. "We will see!"

In his opening statement, the prosecuting attorney, Snook McGee, detailed each charge against the defendants. In his presentation, his words were laced with uncustomary eloquence and flamboyance as he addressed the jury. When he talked, they listened; they laughed; they cried; and they hung on his every word. At the conclusion of his emotion-laced remarks of condemnation, he presented each juror a Peppermint Patty after-dinner mint, just for effect.

"Not only will I demonstrate absolutely convincing evidence for you to condemn these hardened criminals," he summarized, "but when you return to the court your unanimous verdict of guilty, you will each taste that sweet justice that has been served!" He then bowed at the waist, turned and took his seat at the prosecutor's table.

"Damn," Liddiard whispered to his clients. "He's good!"

"Gary! You're supposed to be on our side!" Tyrone reminded his counselor. "I hope you have something better than that to say to the jury!"

"Don't worry," he responded. "I've prepared for this moment my entire life." Gary then stood up and quietly strolled toward the jury box. When passing the judge, he paused and nodded. Not getting a response, he proceeded to within a foot of the jurors.

"I suppose," he began, "you've heard that the two defendants I represent are nervous about trusting their fate to twelve morons who weren't smart enough to get out of jury duty? Ha, ha... just kidding, of course. But seriously, I know jury duty doesn't pay much, but it's likely a huge wage increase for some of you losers! For the others, I'll bet it really seems nice to finally be sitting on this side of the court for a change!

"Hey, yokels," he continued, "here's another good one for you: 'What do you call a lawyer with an IQ of 40? You call him *Your Honor!*' Ha, ha! That's a good one! Well, I've taken a lot of your time and I don't really have much else to say, except that my clients are innocent. Trust me. They really are!"

To the confused looks of Dusty and Ty, Gary returned to his seat and sat down, alternately looking smugly at the jurors and then at the judge, and then back at the jurors.

"We've got 'em right where we want 'em!" Gary whispered to his clients. "I think I made a great opening impression on the jury and the judge!"

The defendants could only manage to roll their eyes in disbelief.

. . .

Prosecutor McGee rose and called his first witness.

"Will Cap'ting Snook McGee please come to the stand?" The prosecutor then crossed over to the witness stand and stood stoically with his hand to the square.

Making an about face and backing up a few steps to again act as the prosecutor, he said "Do you swear to tell the truth, the whole truth and nothing but the truth, so help you God?"

Returning to the witness stand, he raised his right hand and promised "Yeah, I shir do."

He then sat down in the witness chair, looked toward the judge and smiled a toothless smile. After a moment, he staggered down from the witness chair and walked around to the face the bench. Acting the part as both prosecutor *and* witness, he continued to exchange positions after each question and/or answer.

The court stenographer's report reads as follows:

Prosecutor: "Do you recognize the two accused defendants seated across from you… the two that are tethered in chains and shackles over there?" He pointed in the direction of the actors.

Snook: "Yep. They're them Hollywood play actors; Dusty O'Neal 'n Tyrone "T-Bone" Jameson."

Prosecutor: "Where were you two days ago, on Sunday afternoon?"

Snook: "I wuz drivin' a commercial fishin' boat named the *Solstice* up th' Lynn Canal, headed t'ward Juneau. Th' boat b'longs to Mr. Ponch Marchbanks an' I've a'casionally used 'er this summer on a lease 'greement. I seeze 'nother boat that looked sim'lar and pulled over t' take a look. Lo an' b'hold, th' other cat'meran was the spittin' image of the *Solstice*. Th' other'n wuz named th' *Equinox*! Spittin' image!"

Prosecutor: "What happened next?"

Snook: "I'll be damned if those two (pointing at the defendants) didn't force themselves on me for an unpaid fishin' trip!"

Defense Attorney: "Objection, your honor. He's making this up!"

Judge: "Overruled."

Defense Attorney: "Please enter it in the record that I object! This court isn't only deaf and blind... she's also as dumb as an ass!"

Judge: "Sit down counselor, or you'll be held in contempt." (The defense attorney sat down.)

Prosecutor: "Please continue, Cap'ting."

Snook: "The defendants stole beer from m' boat and they drank it. Then they forced me into a card game. One that I'd hardly never play'd b'fore. It wuz 'ginst m' will! They cheated me an' made me put up th' *Solstice* 'ginst their movie royalties. Then they ganged up an' cheated me outa' th' boat."

Prosecutor: "Is that all or is there more, Cap'ting Snook?"

Snook: "There's lots more! Those defendants pulled a knife on me, then one of 'em hit me an' knock'd me overboard. I could'a took th' two uv 'em, even w'out m' knife, but I'd had a little too much t' drink an' I didn't wanna git cut! I swimm'd t' Vanderbilt Reef and staid there a'freezin' 'til a boat came by an' help'd me out. They let me use thir phone an' so I called th' owner of the *Solstice* an' he came an' pick'd me up and brought me back t' safety. He wuz th' real hero in this adventure an' he saved m' life!"

Judge: "From the sounds of it, it appears that the prosecution failed to accuse the defendants of attempted murder. Let it be entered in the record that I reserve the right to add attempted murder to the charges."

Defense Attorney: "You can't do that! Good hell all mighty, judge, are you just making this up as you go?"

Judge: "One more outburst like that, counselor, and I'll hold you in contempt for sure. Now, sit down and shut up!" (The defense attorney sat down.)

The prosecutor then excused the witness and presented the court a number of tagged items for evidence, including a picture of the *Solstice*, a water logged deck of cards, a very sharp saber with a sheath and a cell phone photograph of Snook sitting alone on a rock on the Vanderbilt Reef. The snapshot had been had been taken by Ponch when he arrived in *Sweet Cheeks* to rescue the Cap'ting.

After entering these items into evidence, the prosecutor rested his case.

The Judge called for a ten minute recess to allow everyone to "refresh themselves over the side of the boat," after which the court was called back to order.

Again, we will extract from the court reporter's record:

Defense Attorney: "I'd like to cross examine the previous witness, your honor."

Judge: "Denied. It is a conflict of interest for you to examine the Prosecuting Attorney in this court of law. He holds too much confidential information, details that are only privy to the prosecution. It would be unjust to put him under oath in this situation."

Defense Attorney: "Your honor, what's the difference between a judge and a rockfish?"

Judge: "Well, this doesn't sound like something you should be saying right now, counselor."

Defense Attorney: "One is a bottom-dwelling, garbage-eating scavenger and the other is a fish! I would like to call Dusty O'Neal to the witness stand, your honor!"

The judge was dumbfounded and before he found the words to react, Dusty was standing in front of the witness stand with his hand to the square.

Defense Attorney: "Do you swear to tell the truth, the whole truth and nothing but the truth?"

O'Neal: "I do."

Defense Attorney: "Will you please rehearse your version of what happened between Snook McGee and you and Tyrone on the day in question?"

O'Neal: "Well, yes. It was pretty much like Snook said… except that it was the exact opposite. We didn't force ourselves on his boat. He invited us. We didn't steal his beer, he offered it to us. We didn't cheat at cards, we played fair and square. We didn't pull out a knife. He threatened us and held us captive with his knife until we finally took it away from him. We did force him overboard, though, but only because we knew he would be safe on the rocks until someone came to his rescue."

Defense Attorney: "Do you have a copy of the signed agreement for the wager of the *Solstice* against your movie royalties?"

O'Neal: "No, I don't have it anymore. I lost it to the judge at the poker table a little while ago."

Judge: The judge produced a tattered, hand written note out of his pocket and waived it back and forth in front of the defense attorney. "Is this what you are looking for?"

Defense Attorney: "Yes. That is it! If it pleases the court, I would like to enter that copy of the signed and witnessed gambling agreement into evidence, your honor."

Judge: "Denied. It really doesn't please the court at all. The document belongs to me and therefore, it is privileged."

Defense Attorney: "Seriously?

Judge: "Seriously."

Defense Attorney: "I'd call this a Kangaroo Court, but that's just an insult to kangaroos! I have nothing more to present, so I rest my case."

Judge Marchbanks rapped his gavel three times and ended the proceedings.

"There's no reason for the prosecuting attorney to cross examine this witness," he said, "considering that we've just heard the most pathetic defense ever witnessed. I'm not going to bother asking the jury to adjourn to reach a verdict, since this is pretty much an open and shut case. You guys just talk amongst yourselves for a minute or two and let me know what you decide."

Before they deliberated, Bruce Gordon (the night watchman at the nearby Ocean Beauty Cannery) was elected to be the jury foreman. After the vote, the twelve men huddled together and mumbled to one another for less than a minute. After which, they all laughed and slapped one another on the back.

Jury Foreman Gordon then rose and declared "Both defendants are guilty as sin on all counts, your honor, and we're going to include the attempted murder charge. Furthermore, we the jury, also recommend that their inept counselor serves time with them!"

"Agreed," the Judge asserted. "Take all three of them to the dungeon while I deliberate on their sentence. Keep them in shackles and chains, hanging upside down from the ceiling, until I call for them in the morning. Court is adjourned until tomorrow morning when I will render their sentence.

"Now, everyone! Let's continue our evening of gambling, drinking, smoking and socializing. Yvette and Yvonne, please bring out the fondue for everyone to enjoy while the evening is still young!"

Immediately, with the heavy handed assistance of Jared and Dan, the court bailiff did as ordered.

...

The amount of time spent hanging upside down in shackles could not be discerned by the captives, since they had each passed out and were comatose from the trauma. Awareness returned gradually to all three and then waned from pain to incoherency, then back to pain again.

Occasional, disjointed thoughts flashed through their minds and then faded back to the blackness of unconsciousness. Gathering their collective senses took a significant amount of time and energy.

Finally, Dusty broke the silence: "Man, I didn't see that coming. So much for being on a roll!"

"How do we get out of this mess?" Tyrone managed through his blood, sweat and tears. "By the way, Gary, you're fired! And don't quit your day job! When it comes to lawyering, you're pathetic!"

Gary's response was not discernable, but Dusty thought he heard him say "I swear I thought we had the case in the bag."

Dusty simply shook his head in disbelief.

Each tried in vain to loosen their hands from the straps that bound them tightly to the wall, but to no avail. They strained to pull their legs from the shackles that were holding them upside down from bolts in the ceiling, but again, it was of no use.

Twisting their limbs in the wrist and ankle irons resulted in drawing blood from their already injured extremities. It was a desperate situation and every movement added to their increasing sense of pain.

To make matters worse, a tailless rat darted across the floor and came within a whisker of Ty's head. The shackled prisoner tried to keep his bushy hair from touching the ground by tightening his stomach as he arched to hold up his head. Eventually, however, his abs burned and he gave up the exercise.

Sensing victory, the rat leaped onto the exposed side of his head, scurried up his temple and onto his neck. T-Bone winced and held his breath. The rat paused, then went further, traversing his victim's draping shirt tail until reaching the exposed skin of his belly.

Again, the rodent paused. Ty continued to hold his breath and remained perfectly still. He worried that if he moved or shook to dislodge the rat, he might be bitten.

Ever so slowly, the rat inched upward on Ty's bare skin until reaching his loosely secured denims. Because the handsome actor had been hanging upside down, gaps were created between his skin and pants. The rat surveyed his opportunities.

With his head and ears simultaneously stiffened, the rat then stood erect and sniffed in all directions while considering his options.

A flash of dread came into Tyrone's mind when he remembered the partially eaten ham and Swiss cheese remaining from his *Lunchables* snack. The leftovers had been deposited in his right pocket, awaiting future consumption.

The whiskered rodent stood poised on the left side of Ty's belly when he detected the smell of the ripening ham and cheese. Within a breath of time, the rat darted inside the space between the trousers and his benefactor's abdomen. He then proceeded gingerly across the actor's pelvis. Tyrone stiffened and held his breath while the rat moved slowly and deliberately across his crotch and then up his right pant leg; then ever so carefully to where the inner pocket was tightly pressed against his leg.

Ty recognized that he was entering panic mode and began experiencing sweat from fear that began oozing from his every pore. He could feel the varmint scratching and moving in a circular motion, as if in the process of building a nest.

Each time the rat moved, Tyrone twitched. His only defense was to keep twitching until (he hoped) the rat would give up on his ham and cheese expedition.

After an exceptionally exaggerated twitch, the rat bit down fiercely into the soft skin near Ty's crotch and then darted up his thigh toward daylight at the pant leg opening. To Tyrone's relief, the intruder made his exit across his stocking and shoe and then scrambled up the chain that was shackled to his ankle. Ty continued to hold his breath until he saw the rat disappear through a small crevice in the wooden wall of the vessel.

. . .

After lying still for what seemed to be an eternity, the threesome heard loud noises that increased to crashing mayhem in the room directly above them. The sounds escalated until they reached riot proportions. In a quick exchange, they realized that they were hanging in shackles directly beneath the casino, where they could hear men shouting in terror. From the cracking and reverberating disaster sounding overhead, they imagined the bodies of their captors were being thrown overboard in the chaos. They strained to see through the small porthole opening in their otherwise dark and dingy prison, but could not discern what was happening.

Suddenly, the source of the mayhem presented itself squarely in the entrance of the ship's dungeon. The galley door was filled with the outline of a beast they immediately recognized. It was the horrific form of Kustaka. There was no mistaking the pungent odor that invariably preceded his presence.

The behemoth emitted a mighty roar as he savagely ripped the trim off the door, allowing him space to enter the small dungeon.

Gary promptly fainted from the calamitous episode. Dusty and Tyrone remained conscious, but were both seized with terror as the mangy beast burst into their prison chamber. They grimaced and shut their eyes tightly as he drew nearer and nearer to them. In unison, both sensed that impending death and dismemberment were looming on the horizon. They feared their time on earth was about to come to a grizzly end.

Shackles and chains flew wildly in the small, lower level dungeon when Kustaka popped the tie down bolts out of the wall with his bare hands. Immediately, Dusty (and shortly thereafter, Tyrone) marveled as the beast freed the three men from their upside down hanging position with what could only be described as gentle power.

Once Gary was revived and all three were resting on their backs on the plank floor, the hairy animal painstakingly pried the shackles open for each of them. The animal took precaution to avoid even so much as a slight pinch to the bruised and scraped wrists and ankles of the tortured prisoners.

The compassion in the beast's large brown eyes was evident and the freed captives thought they could detect a slight smile on his thick, large lips. They patted his arm as he worked, wanting to show gratitude for his timely rescue.

After finishing his work, the animal stood erect and roared, sending them back into a muddle of fearful confusion for their physical safety. Nevertheless, they continued to patronize him as they made their way up the short spiral stairwell and out of the dungeon. Intrepidly, they entered the casino, which now looked like a trailer park after a hurricane.

Working their way through the debris and destruction as they followed Kustaka, they located an outside door and made their escape to freedom. The door exited adjacent to the entrance of the ship's poop deck, at the rear of the *Rig*.

Unexpectedly, the *Solstice* was still bobbing near the *Rig*, right where Dusty and Tyrone had anchored her earlier in the evening.

"Hell, I'm glad we don't have to swim back to the lodge!" Ty joked. "We'd die from hypothermia after a minute or two in this ice cold water. I honestly thought that crooked judge and his minions would have taken the catamaran with them."

"They would have if they hadn't left in such a big hurry!" Dusty answered.

Right at the moment when he finished his sentence, the men heard a loud splash from what sounded like an exaggerated belly flop. They turned just in time to see Kustaka disappear into the icy deep. All three stared in unbelief as the hairy beast vanished into the darkness of the deep water.

Quietly but quickly, the men reeled in the tether rope and boarded the *Solstice*. With unblinking focus, the reformed gamblers sped across the inlet toward the relative safety of the *Alaskan Bear Lodge* while the floating casino remained anchored above the Russian Hump.

For Dusty, Ty and Gary, the vessel's proximity to the lodge was fortuitous. Their trip home was short and the lodge's lights served as a beacon for them. Even though the ride took less than five minutes by boat, it would have been an impossible distance for them to swim, even if the water was not at its usual frigid temperature.

The late evening breeze blew wildly through the boaters' hair as they wondered aloud to one another what might have become of the men who had vacated the *Rig* under duress.

• • •

Meanwhile, back on deck... or more exactly, under the rough sawn wooden canopy which was thoughtfully designed to shelter poop deck patrons from inclement weather, six unblinking eyes gaped silently. With the glaring stealth of cats on the prowl, they watched as the final humans and the unthinkable beast abandoned the *Rig*. Finally at ease when he was sure no one was left onboard, Randazzle loosened his protective arm lock on each of the frightened bar maids who had found safety in his masculine grasp during the mayhem.

Breaking the silence, he spoke to the twins, "I want my credit cards back," he sneered. "...and what were you two thinking, getting yourselves mixed up with this rowdy crowd?"

"I can hardly breathe in this smelly little cubbyhole," gushed Yvonne, attempting to dodge an awkward question. "Is it safe to go outside now?"

"Yes. I think everyone has jumped ship," Randazzle smiled broadly. "Now it's just the three of us. We're alone at last!" His sinister sneer was visible through his thick, chemically darkened mustache and his lecherous intentions were not lost on the girls.

"Yvonne is right," Yvette said firmly as she pressed her sharp, boney elbow into his kidney. "Let us out of this cesspool right now!"

"Ok. But first, where are my credit cards, driver's license and my cell phone?"

"They're probably right where we left them... in the bottom of your fly rod case!"

"You two are unbelievable," Randazzle laughed in disgust. He was visibly relieved that his belongings had not been mailed to his wife. The relief he felt caused him to make the first wise decision of his vacation when he decided to back away and not press his luck with the girls.

"Ok. Let's get out of this cage and back into the fresh air. If we go out one at a time, I think we can squeeze through. Easy does it."

When everyone was on deck, they spotted the lights shining from the lodge on the opposite side of the inlet. Looking north, they also saw bright, variegated colors in the sky. They were pleasantly surprised that the Aurora Borealis' indescribable reflections of romantic colors and light are often seen on crisp, clear nights at the headwaters of Excursion Inlet.

Deep in thought, Randazzle sighed and muttered under his breath, "What lousy luck. If these babes only knew what they were missing."

"What are you saying?" Yvette asked, thinking the aging dentist was quietly articulating a way for them to cross the inlet.

"I was saying, let's look around and find the skiff at the front of the boat," he said, as if that was what he had been mumbling all along. "I remember seeing one tied up on the deck when I boarded."

When they arrived at the fore deck, the trio was relieved that his memory was correct. They worked together to gently lower the small aluminum dinghy with the name *Fish 'n Chips* scrawled on the side, down and into the water. One at a time, they stepped gingerly into the skiff, hoping it would not tip or sink once all were aboard.

Using a small, broken oar found on the floor, Randazzle quietly and gently paddled the little boat and the twins toward the inviting night lights shining from the distant cabin.

CHAPTER FIFTEEN

THE PLOT THICKENS

Wednesday morning's breakfast was the first occasion that all eight *Alaskan Bear Lodge* fishing guests were together at one location. Dusty O'Neal, Tyrone Jameson, Gary Liddiard and Dr. Franklin Hulme constituted four of the eight; the other campers, who arrived by floatplane before breakfast was served, were Jeremy Trail and Shawn Ford, a pair of practical joking risk managers from Utah and Dr. Karl Nielsen, a noted Utah neurosurgeon.

The eighth guest in the group was Peter VanTassle an outwardly ordinary middle aged man whose bank account was much deeper than his shallow personality. Being without friend or companion, he had signed on to come to the fishing lodge alone.

VanTassle habitually puffed on his pipe, all the while peering down his large nose as he condescendingly patronized others. He spoke with a loud and exaggerated Dutch accent and constantly interrupted and corrected the others. His aura was

that of a self-absorbed, conceited man who continually suggested that he knew every detail about everything.

After the lodge keeper read "The Rules of the Camp" to the
group, he sensed his hands would be full with this dysfunctional
mixture of guests. A tightening knot formed in his stomach as he
considered idea after idea to mold the eclectic group of fishermen
into a mutually enjoyable society of peers. It would not be easy.

Late the previous night, however, Devin McMichaels felt he
was the recipient of divine intervention as he watched Yvette and
Yvonne Svendsen being rowed ashore by their would-be para-
mour, Dr. Hulme.

When they inquired about the possibility of becoming the
lodge's domestic aids for a few weeks, he knew providence was
smiling down upon him. What he did not know was that the girls
were primarily seeking protection from their lecherous old
predator while they earned enough money to return to the safety
of their parents in Petersburg.

Because there was very little local help for hire during tourist
season, the lodge had adopted a system of providing guests their
accommodations and meals with no staff for cooking, washing
dishes or cleaning rooms. Of necessity, the lodge operated as a top
of the line do-it-yourself fishing camp. Surprisingly, after experiencing the process, most campers would not have their fishing
week in the remote climes of Alaska any other way.

Following the group meeting in which he explained the camp
rules, the lodge keeper's job reduced to one similar to an orchestra
conductor: He instructed, monitored and, in general, did whatever
he could to create harmony within his group of adventurers. He
was expected to do no more and no less.

As Wednesday progressed, it was evident to Devin that he
might be in over his head with the personalities making up the
week's guest list. Experiencing the quirks of half of his guests the
day before the others arrived, he could see that problems might

soon form on the horizon. The lodge keeper discerned that he would need to be inventive in order to deal with the biggest shirk and chronic grumbler of the summer: the obnoxious Dutchman.

As a whole, the entire group complained less of aches and pains than did the friendless VanTassle. Not once did he volunteer for any of the petty duties required of the campers: a bucket of water to be brought; an armful of wood to be chopped; clutter to straighten up, and so forth. The European constantly complained about one thing or another: a sprain, a blister, not enough hot water, needing a fresh dry towel, and any number of other maladies or inconveniences that needed special attention.

VanTassle was first to turn in at night, even when a score of tasks remained to be done. Yet, he was the last to rise each morning when there were duties to execute before breakfast had begun. He was at the front of the serving line at mealtime, yet he never helped wash and dry dishes afterward.

It was customary each morning for a couple men to board and row the lodge's aluminum skiff from the shore to the floating dock in order to haul the day's supply of poles and gear to the fishing boats. When it was VanTassle's turn, he slyly cut the water at each stroke and allowed the skiff's momentum to float above his oar, making it seem like he was rowing. As was his style, he often put forth more effort to avoid work than he would have expended by actually performing the task at hand.

Self-indulged, Peter thought no one noticed his sly tricks, but the other fishermen increasingly swore under their breath and grew to despise him. Dr. Nielsen, his assigned roommate, soon started to openly sneer and curse him, believing he was nothing more than a boorish pretender. Recriminations, however, did not phase the foreigner. Instead, they served to make him even more brazen.

In utter exasperation, after he spent a day in captivity on the fishing boat with VanTassle, Nielsen called a secret meeting with the other lodgers to devise a scheme to neutralize the object of his disgust. If for no other reason, his plot was being brewed as a device to get through the week with his sanity (which was now borderline) still in check.

After he explained his scheme, the lodge keeper and the other guests heartily joined Dr. Nielsen's prank. Dusty and Ty, however, declined participation, saying their personal drama during the past couple days had been enough to fill their appetite without intentionally adding more.

Of the group, only the haughty Peter VanTassle was clueless as to what mischievous intrigue was being hatched on his behalf for the near future.

■ ■ ■

The night before the lodge's guests convened for breakfast, one after another of Ponch's band of brothers assembled about a mile south of the mouth of Excursion Inlet, at the *Salmon Run Lodge*.

The iconic lodge, with its distinctive red metal roof, was large enough to house all *Brotherhood* comers. The large great room was ideal for planning meetings and the cozy beds and warm showers were an attractive amenity that provided the men a much needed respite from their exhaustion. Physically, the activities of the past few days had taken their toll.

While some of the men were merely fatigued, a few were wet and chilled to the bone from having spent time in the freezing waters during their hasty retreat from the *Rig*. All had the look of "blood in their eye" for the outsiders who were collectively and individually to blame for the chain of events of the past few days.

"I sez we torch thir boats an' thir lodge!" slurred McGee. "I ain't nev'r bin treated sa' poorly!"

"You're a damned firebug, Snook, and you got what was comin' to you," Ponch replied. "If you wasn't so damned greedy, you'd do better in the long run. Now let's quit lickin' our wounds. I'm calling this meeting of the *Brotherhood* to order. Everybody sit down and listen up!" After reciting the fraternity motto ("Whatever it takes; whatever it takes!") in unison, the men formed their chairs in a semi-circle and sat, listening intently to their leader.

Since Excursion Inlet is so far from civilization, there is very little (if any) formal law enforcement to keep unprincipled rascals in line. Andy Torgensen, locally known as an outstanding Alaska wildlife trooper, was the only sworn officer who was assigned patrol in and around the remote stretches of the Icy Strait. Although he was efficient and dedicated, he was stretched to the limit in his efforts to enforce law enforcement in such a vast and out of the way part of the world.

One fraternal brother or another was always on assignment to know the whereabouts of officer Andy and was further charged with keeping Ponch fully apprised at all times. On this particular evening, it was reported that Torgensen was at leisure on the opposite side of the Icy Strait. He was home in Hoonah where he was enjoying a hot evening meal with his family, while getting some much overdue rest from his work.

After initiating the meeting, Ponch opened the floor to orderly and well considered suggestions to "roust out these intruders from our sacred fishing waters. This nefarious band of interlopers needs to return to the lower forty-eight with some hair raising tales about their time in the Icy Strait."

"I still sez we should burn 'em out!" McGee again suggested. "A good fire is always fun an' I'd bet they'd take that story home with 'em!"

"Sit down and shut up," Ponch ordered. "Snook, you're a regular pyromaniac... we're not goin' down that road again! Two torch jobs this week ought to be enough. You've had your fire works for the month!"

After more thoughtful suggestions were presented from several of the men, they voted and unitedly settled on a well devised plot proposed by Keith Skaflestad. The Master then ended the meeting, after which three partially refreshed men were assigned to board the *Karen Marie* with Keith. Together they sped out to sea to lay the ground work to put Keith's plan into action.

Instead of going with the others, Jared was dispatched across the Icy Strait to Hoonah to set in motion his part of the scheme.

The *Karen Marie* streaked toward Point Adolphus, near the northern shores of Chichigof Island, and the four comrades busied themselves by unraveling Skaflestad's halibut skate. To be heard above the roar of the twin Yamaha 250 motors (both torqued to the limit of their capacity) they yelled loudly to one another in colorful seaman vocabulary.

The men were back on the water on a high adventure mission and were once again in their element.

It was not a night at sea for the faint of heart, nor for the faint of strength. Collectively and individually, the *Brotherhood* was thorough in preparing themselves to carry out Skaflestad's conspiracy.

CHAPTER SIXTEEN

COHO TROLLING

G ary could not have been happier. He was finally enjoying a perfect day, trolling for Coho Salmon between Home Shore and the Log Dump in a twenty four foot aluminum trolling boat. He was a few miles south of the lodge and, as it is everywhere throughout southeast Alaska, the scenery was spectacular.

Rugged, snowcapped mountains shot out of the sea at the shoreline and the series of dramatic peaks that rose steeply above the water were divided by deep canyons. The valley closest to his fishing location was formed and defined by centuries of runoff flowing into creek carved ravines that ultimately emptied into Windy River. The freshet flowed gracefully from the top of the mountains down to the sea below.

Rising to the west, the Fair Weather Mountains were a distant purple. Light clouds breezed by alternately covering and revealing the rugged Sitka spruce on both sides of the Inlet. On occasion, the clouds hovered above the seawater, just a short distance beyond where he was fishing. He felt the recurring gentle mist from the passing clouds, but there was not enough moisture for him to consider it to be rain.

Periodically, a loud boom was heard, followed by a distant gusher from the blow hole of a humpback whale. All the while, eagles soared overhead in abundance, looking for food to snatch from the water below. Heaven could not possibly be an improvement on this place, he brooded.

"There are no river rafters around to torpedo the serenity of my fishing day," he thankfully contemplated. Reverently, he reflected about how much he enjoyed the quiet company of his fishing companions. All three were mesmerized in a sleepy trance. He was grateful, he thought out loud, that he did not have to suffer by listening to the constant complaining and self-promoting diatribe of Peter VanTassle on such a beautiful day.

"Any time now," Liddiard softly intoned to the others, "I expect that blasted European will finish his ongoing commentary with *'But enough about me.... what do you think about me?'*"

"Ha!" smiled Dr. Nielsen. "That really is funny, Gary! I was just thinking about how nice it's been to be away from that unimaginative dolt! Don't give up on your thoughts, though. There's sufficient time left back at the lodge for VanTassle to start trolling for compliments. It's good that I brought earplugs to the lodge or I wouldn't get a minute of sleep. In addition to bragging and complaining, he snores like a freight train! Do any of you care to switch roommates with me?"

Shawn and Jeremy joined in. "I feel sorry for the two actors fishing with him today," Shawn confessed. "They're probably certifiable by now. The man is a tedious, mind numbing bore!"

"Yeah, and the poor dentist has to be suffering, too," Jeremy added. "I'll bet he wishes he could trade VanTassle for those two babes he brought to the lodge last night. Swapping their company for that old know-it-all was a giant step in the wrong direction, if you ask me!"

150

"Fish on!" Liddiard shouted abruptly. "No... TWO FISH ON! Grab your poles and bring in the other lines so we don't get tangled. Mine is running like a monster!"

All four men sprung into action. The insurance agents reeled in their lines and, when completed, Ford grabbed the over-sized fishing net to assist in the catch. Liddiard and Nielsen fought their prey with deft experience. "Rod up! Reel down the line!" encouraged Jeremy.

"Keep 'im in the water," instructed Shawn. "I'll net 'im. He's gettin' close!"

As soon as Liddiard's salmon was secured and pulled into the boat, Karl started screaming for the net. "Get over here, pronto! I don't know if I can keep him on the line much longer!"

"Hang in there, Doc!" Shawn shouted. "Gary's hook is tangled in the net! Keep your fish in the water and I'll have the hook out of the net shortly!"

"Damn and double damn! My trophy just got some slack and jerked himself off of the hook! Damnit! That was one huge Coho, too!"

"Sorry, Doc. These double hook-ups are tough when the net gets tangled. Sorry, friend."

"If it's any consolation, Doc, I'll give you the honor of stunning my Coho," Liddiard offered. "Grab the bat and swing away!"

Nielsen seized the small bat and took out his frustrations by teeing off on Liddiard's Silver salmon, hitting it squarely between the eyes. "Easy, big guy!" Liddiard cautioned. "I'd rather not eat bruised salmon, if you don't mind! I think you've finished him off."

"Get the lines back into the water," Nielsen ordered. "I'll be catching *and* netting the next big fish. Just watch and learn!"

"It can't possibly get any better than this," mused Liddiard aloud. "I love Alaska!"

. . .

Meanwhile, a few miles across the channel, the tired and angry men of the fraternal order were methodically setting their second halibut skate in the productive fishing waters just off the shore of Point Adolphus. They worked well together, without anyone saying much to the others. Their sneaky, underhanded plan was foolproof and they knew it was a winner.

At home in Hoonah, Officer Torgensen felt lethargic and sluggish after finishing his second large helping at the dinner table. During several trying days of law enforcement in remote Alaska, he had suffered his assignments alone and was happily contemplating a few days of well-earned rest.

Less than a mile from Andy's home, Jared checked into one of the small sleeping rooms at the *Icy Strait Lodge*. After getting settled, he walked down the hallway past the lobby and into the lounge. Once inside the dimly lit dining room that doubled as a bar, Jared ordered a baked Alaskan halibut dinner and a six pack of cold beer.

. . .

Fishing near the Log Dump, Randazzle, Dusty and Tyrone each felt as if their heads were about to explode after listening to Peter rave on and on about himself and his implausible exploits. They heard all they could mentally manage and then nodded toward one another. The decision was universal, so they reeled in their lines, fully engaged their ninety horsepower Johnson and made a beeline for the lodge. They were mentally exhausted.

"I'm going to join Doc Nielsen's plot to put VanTassle in his place," Dusty discretely whispered to Ty. "I completely underestimated how trite and emotionally draining this thickheaded half-wit is."

"Yeah. Me too," Tyrone replied. "Me too."

●●●

Skaflestad and his helpers worked tirelessly, unraveling and dropping down the well baited halibut skate. "Stretch the line along the half circle I'm making with the boat," he instructed. "Watch for tangles. We want to pull out a massive catch of halibut in the morning!"

The men worked with a unified purpose at a feverous pace. "Those gol' dang'd sport fishers'll wish they'd never come to th' Icy Strait," Snook hissed to no one in particular. "They'll larn t' mess with us locals!"

The skate was set and buoys were arranged in record time. Then the *Karen Marie* sped toward Ponch's place in Gustavus with the band of conspirators. After tying to the dock, all four piled into Ponch's pick up. Snook sat comfortably on the worn out seat in the cab next to Ponch, who was behind the steering wheel and Skaflestad chose to sit in the back of the truck, where he could stretch his legs. He soon regretted his choice, however, since it became a bouncing, bumpy ride on the hard flooring as they wound their way through pothole after pothole on their way to Ponch's compound.

Once they arrived, all four went inside the cabin and Ponch promptly placed a call to the *Icy Strait Lodge,* asking for Jared Long. After delays lasting several minutes, Jared was located in the lounge and was summoned to the phone.

"Is the skate set?" he asked Ponch.

"Both skates are baited and set," the Master replied. "We're at my place, but we're goin' to the *Glacier Bay Lodge* for dinner. Stay there at the *Icy Strait* where I can reach you by phone when we've finished our part of the job."

"Will do," Long replied. "I'll stay right here in the bar all night, if you want! It's nice 'n warm here and I'm plenty thirsty."

After enjoying a hearty dinner, the Alaskans returned to Ponch's home where they milled around in the bachelor quarters until each found a private sleeping corner. They curled up in sleeping bags, using blankets for mattresses, and immediately fell asleep. The men slept deeply for almost five hours, while the time passed for Skaflestad's skate nets to fill with halibut.

CHAPTER SEVENTEEN

THE SET-UP

D r. Nielsen had long since fulfilled his goals as a successful big game hunter. His elaborate home in a high mountain valley of the Wasatch Range could easily be mistaken for a wildlife museum.

Much to his wife's chagrin, every room of their residence was filled with head mounts, racks and full body mounts, representing beasts of every kind and description. The world renowned neurosurgeon had brought home bounty from numerous African safaris, as well as from his many years of big game hunts across North and South America and beyond. If it walked, Nielsen had bagged it.

Over a pot roast and scalloped potato dinner, the Doc enlivened the conversation with stories of his most exotic hunts. Even the "one-ups-manship" comments of the ever annoying Peter VanTassle were endured and, as it seemed, even encouraged by the others.

Lodge keeper McMichaels had a sense that camaraderie might be settling in, albeit at the expense of their new found common nuisance. For that, he breathed a noticeable sigh of relief. "Bonding," he thought, 'for whatever reason, is still bonding. A friendship or two in this mix-matched group just might form after all."

"Ah, yes," VanTassle nodded in condescension to everyone in the room. In his thick accent, he acknowledged "I vas on safari myself az a very young man. My marksmanship vas zo keen, I vunce downed both a zebra and ze lion vat vaz attacking it vith ze zingle shot!"

"Really," Randazzle replied. "As well as an expert marksman, you must have made some lightening quick geometry calculations!"

"Ah, yes," continued VanTassle. "My keen intellect not only gained me my Juris Doctor degree from ze University of Amsterdam, but, I vas also at ze top of my geometry class. I can calculate ze complicated geometric problems vith ze lightning speed! It eez common knowledge that I have a genius I.Q. Ve Europeans av' long bin known to be intellectually zuperior over ze Americans."

"I once heard that," Dusty patronized. "I wonder why that is so?"

"It iz a vedy zimple explanation. I vill speak in elementary terms so zat each of you vill understand. Ve first must consider ze difference between ze pure bred canines and ze common mutts. I need not provide scientific documentation for you to recognize zee mental and physical advantage zat ze pure bred dog enjoys over ze mutt. Ze zame is true in ze humans. Americans, although zey try to compete vith ze pure breds, are zimply a diluted race. Vedy few purebreds are left in America. Pardon ze expression, but most of your countrymen are ze mutts and, ergo, are inferior intellectually and physically to ze Europeans. It is ze known fact!"

"That explains a lot. Thank you, Peter," muttered T-Bone humbly while rolling his eyes. As an afterthought, he continue, "I would really like to see you shoot, if that wouldn't be too much to ask."

"Ah, but of course. I vould be most happy to demonstrate my zuperior firearm skills. It iz too bad ve are in zuch ze remote location and without access to ze weaponry," Peter apologized. "Othervise... vell, another time, another place. I could eezily instruct all of you, including you, Dr. Nielsen, on ze finer points of ze marksmanship."

"This is your lucky day, Mr. VanTassle!" the lodge keeper's voice boomed from the kitchen. He appeared at the dining room entrance and continued, "The owner of the lodge brought me a shotgun and skeet thrower last spring. I will have it set up for you in no time at all!"

"But... but..." VanTassle objected. "But..."

"No buts about it, Peter. It really is no trouble at all. I can have the equipment set up in about ten minutes. After you've enjoyed dessert, we will go outside and shoot off the sea wall, right in front of the lodge."

"It's settled, then! Peter will treat us to a 'zuperier' skeet shooting exhibition," Gary confirmed, tongue-in-cheek. "'Zuperior!'"

"Here, here!" added Ford.

Trapped from all sides, Peter slowly finished eating his pot roast and grudgingly consented to the proposed skeet shooting challenge.

After enjoying a mix of chocolate and vanilla pudding for dessert (a traditional *Alaskan Bear Lodge* speciality) the sportfishing guests removed themselves to the seawall in front of the lodge. The lodge keeper had set up the skeet throwing apparatus and the shotgun and ammunition were ready for the demonstration.

"Our timing is perfect," Devin informed the enthusiastic contingent huddling near the thrower. "It's almost high tide. I prefer to have our guests shoot at high tide. That way, when the tide recedes, I can retrieve the clay pigeons that weren't hit. I can reuse them. They plop into the water and gently settle to the bottom, unbroken and as good as new."

"Man, you're a cheapskate," Gary ribbed. "I hope you don't reuse everything! Come to think of it, the toilet paper upstairs looked a little soiled."

From the vantage point where he sat alone on the deck, above and behind the skeet setup, Dr. Nielsen joined the conversation. "You don't have to worry, Dev. When Mr. VanTassle shoots, there won't be much left of your pigeons!" Hiding his half smile by placing his hand over his mouth and chin while speaking, he continued, "No doubt, we could throw two pigeons out at once and he'd hit 'em both with one shot!"

Looking nervous and unsure of himself, a posture hitherto unexpressed by the unabashed self-promoter, Peter sheepishly proposed his alibi, "Vell... it haz been quite ze while zince I held a firearm."

"I must apologize to you, Peter," McMichaels smiled as he handed the 20-gage to the European. "This Winchester is all we have, and as I'm sure you already know, Winchesters are American made shotguns. Good luck. I hope it doesn't backfire on you!"

VanTassle timidly handled the shotgun, pensively testing its weight and balance. With his confidence gradually increasing, he sighted in over the water, squinting and looking down the barrel until he felt that he was as comfortable as he was going to get.

"Let's get to shooting," Liddiard encouraged. "I've got the video application opened on my cell phone. I'll record your success... but we need to get started. My battery is running low."

After scowling at Gary, Peter put the shotgun to his shoulder and shouted "PULL!"

McMichaels pulled the release and a small orange saucer flew out of the thrower, soaring in an arc over Excursion Inlet's expanse of water.

"Bang!" the gun reported as VanTassle pulled the trigger.

"There's a lucky pigeon that'll live to see tomorrow," Liddiard laughed as the clay pigeon escaped unscathed. "And the high tide saved its life to be used on yet another day!"

"Vell, you may laugh now," VanTassle scowled toward Liddiard. "I'm just sighting in the gun. PULL!"

"Bang!" Again, the pigeon fell to the water untouched.

Frightened by the noise, a pair of eagles soared from the top of a nearby pine tree and swooped over the water, directly into the skeet shooter's line of fire.

Unaware of the birds, VanTassle demanded "PULL!" yet a third time.

"Bang! ...Bang!" History repeated a third time as the clay pigeon fell into the water untouched. To the horror of the shooter, however, both eagles momentarily froze in mid-air and then, uncontrollably, fluttered downward, splashing hard as they hit the water.

"Thaaa...t's not good," Devin slowly drawled. "You might find yourself doing time in an American slammer for dropping eagles out of the sky. I'm sure you know that the eagle is America's national bird and is protected by federal law, don't you, Peter?"

There was no response from the shooter. Just a gaping look of confusion, bewilderment and disbelief.

"Man! What were you thinking, VanTassle?" Shawn yelled from the bench where he and Jeremy sat during the proceedings. "I have to tell you, man, Gary wasn't the only one videoing that massacre. Jeremy also captured your indiscriminate eagle slaughter on camera. It's very clear that you're the sharpshooter you bragged to be and those two dead eagles are proof!"

"Vat, I only took but the vun shot," Peter finally managed to stutter.

"I heard two shots," Randazzle corrected. "The Winchester holds five rounds. I know because I loaded them myself. How many shells are left?"

VanTassle ejected one shell, rendering the chamber and clip empty.

"Apparently, you shot twice, Peter. The shell you ejected, your two previous shots, plus the two you spent killing those eagles. That equals the five shells I loaded into the shotgun. With all the spent shells left cluttering the ground from former shooters, there's no chance to sort out which ones were yours. You took four shots and the last two plucked those two birds right out of the sky!

"We're very proud of the eagle, since it's the symbol of our nation." Randazzle continued. "This has to be reported to the authorities!"

"No! No, please. It vas an accident. I only shot vunce! Please, can't ve just zay nothing. Be reasonable. No one vill know."

"I really don't think so, Mr. VanTassle. We Americans might be mutts, but we have pride in our country! I'll have to report this."

Peter pleaded to the point of sobbing openly, but there was no mercy shown from any of the lodgers. Even the lodge keeper and his comely domestic aides remained stone-faced. For the fishermen, skeet shooting had taken an interesting turn; one that had established intense leverage for them over their annoying nemesis.

Quietly and without fanfare, from where he was partially concealed on the deck, Dr. Nielsen slipped back inside, where he returned the lodge's other shotgun into its case and slid it back to its hiding place under the lodge keeper's bed.

CHAPTER EIGHTEEN

THE SHAKEDOWN

W ake up, Ponch! It's time for us to go pull the nets. The halibut have had plenty of time to get hooked up in the skate!"

"Jeeze Keith. It's four in the morning. Give us another hour!"

"Ponch, it'll take some time to get back to Point Adolphus and then even more time to get my skates pulled up. It's a lot of work! Then, it'll take another forty five minutes to an hour to get back to Excursion with the halibut. We need to leave now if we're going to pull this off before those sport fishers get up!"

"Ok. Ok. I'll put on some coffee and then we'll be on our way. You go wake up th' others."

Ponch rolled out of his bunk and drowsily got dressed. That is to say, if pulling a second fleece over already heavily layered clothing constitutes "getting dressed."

A southeasterly gale had commenced blowing during the night and a heavy storm was rapidly rolling in behind the winds. The seas were cresting at four feet and the marine radio was forecasting a rough sea with increasingly heavy rain in the immediate future. Recommendations were to stay off the water.

Outwardly, the experienced seamen were confident. Without mentioning it to the others, however, each inwardly felt the stomach butterflies that often preceded adventuring into the dangers of the unknown. They knew that many a ship had been lost in calmer waters than the ones they were about to face.

When they were on the boat and had summoned enough testosterone to yell encouragement over the noise of the water craft, Skaflestad insisted that "this kind of weather is ideal for our plans. The landlubbers'll stay in their bunks later than usual this morning, which gives us more time to finish our set up."

"Yer right, Keith," injected Snook. "'Its prob'ly good, after all, that we didn't set fire t' their place. The gale would'a jist blown it out by now anyways."

Controlling the *Karen Marie* in unseasonably bad weather was a greater challenge than the men anticipated. Pulling the heavy skate from the water and extracting one oversized halibut after another, along with a nine foot shark and two sting rays, taxed the men's strength and skill to the limit. It was also a concern to them to keep the ropes from getting tangled in the propellers.

Each man continued the struggle by tapping deeply into his personal pride. Although the fishermen felt strongly compelled to perpetuate their inner macho myth in the eyes of their peers, their individual confidence began to wane. The increasing storm made safety an issue.

Yelling gruff, manly encouragement to one another got them through the ordeal. Ultimately, the skate, along with twenty six halibut, and an impressive selection from other sea life species, were piled high inside the *Karen Marie*. The catch was so voluminous that there remained very little room on deck for the men to stand and Skaflestad's magnificent boat creaked loudly under the weight of the catch.

"This ol' tug a yers gunna make it to 'Scursion?" McGee queried Skaflestad.

"If she does, it'll be a new record," the captain laughed. "And if she don't, it won't surprise me."

"Comferting," Ponch replied. "Real comferting."

It took almost an hour before the passengers of the *Karen Marie* rounded the southeastern tip of Pleasant Island and were able to spot the silver roof of the *Alaskan Bear Lodge*. With high seas and patchy billows of fog, the otherwise easy to sight roof was intermittently in and out of view of the crew's collective naked eye. Mostly, however, it was out of view.

As the vessel drew nearer to the cabin, the absence of yellow glowing house lights encouraged the Alaskans.

"Once again, providence and Mother Nature are on our side," Skaflestad bragged. "She's given us extra cover so's we kin git our chores done!"

With the seas now cresting at five feet, the *Karen Marie* pulled behind the lodge's small fleet of fishing boats. With the skill that comes only from years of experience, the men disembarked and tethered her to the side of the *Filet & Release*. McGee deftly boarded the *Filet* and secured the tie down.

Quickly and quietly, Marchbanks and Skaflestad passed halibut after halibut to their accomplice, who, in turn, stacked the fish into the fish hold and into every nook and cranny on the boat, including piling them deeply into the enclosed cabin.

The *Filet & Release* was filled with an abundant cache of Alaska's finest halibut. For good measure, Skaflestad hauled one additional critter from his boat into the *Filet*. It was a marine animal that, if found in a sport fisherman's possession, was guaranteed to compound their increasing list of manufactured legal problems.

As quietly as she was smuggled in on the rough seas, the *Karen Marie* slipped away into the receding night and traveled southward to the friendly dock at the *Salmon Run,* where the Benevolent Master could make his important phone call to Jared Long.

• • •

Devin McMichaels was not used to hearing the sound of someone knocking on the front door of his lodge. Initially, he thought he was dreaming, but the loud and continuous rapping brought him from his deep sleep back to consciousness.

Observing that a fierce gale was blowing outside, he first thought that a section of tin had come loose on the roof and was banging wildly in the wind. Finally, though, he staggered out of his bed, wandered to the loft overlooking the great room and found his way down the spiral stairs. He was standing at the entrance door, confused and disoriented, when he heard an official directive from outside.

"Open up, immediately!" came the order from the other side of the door. "I'm Wildlife Officer Andy Torgensen. Open the door immediately or risk arrest!"

The lodge keeper cautiously peered through the window. Finally, confident with who was standing on the other side, he proceeded to slowly open the door.

Peeking through the narrow opening, he asked "What's wrong, officer. Is there an emergency?"

"Is the *Filet & Release* one of your boats?"

"Yes, sir, it is. Is there a problem?"

"Yes, there is. Do you mind if I come in out of the weather?" McMichaels complied by opening the door just wide enough for the officer to slide through the gap. Then he closed it and securely fastened the latch.

"How many guests do you have? …and who fished on the *Filet & Release* yesterday?" the officer queried. "Get your guests in here immediately, along with their fishing licenses."

"Yes, sir. But first, can you at least tell me why?"

"Just get them here, pronto! I have no intentions of going through this more than once!"

McMichaels went from room to room, first knocking and then opening each bedroom door. He informed each guest that they must come to the great room immediately, and that they were required to bring their fishing license with them.

The lodgers were at various stages of unconsciousness, but one-by-one they complied with Devin's instructions. Only Peter VanTassle made things difficult. "Vat is da meaning of dis? Dis is an outrage! Are we living in ze Nazi Germany? I demand ze explanation! *I did not shoot doze birds!*"

"Just get your lazy butt out of bed, Peter! Grab your fishing license and drag your sorry ol' bag of bones to the great room," his awakening roommate ordered. Clearly, Dr. Nielsen had reached a boiling point when it came to hearing complaints from the self-centered European.

"Get out there now or I'll throw you out!" he commanded. "And since he's asking for fishing licenses, I doubt this has anything to do with your damned dead eagles."

When all of the men were assembled in the great room, Devin invited Officer Torgensen to step further inside. He was dripping wet from the tempest outside and was visibly relieved to be allowed to take off his rain gear and boots. The puddle he had made on the floor was significant enough to draw a scowl from the lodge keeper.

"Please, state your business, sir," McMichaels requested. "Otherwise, I now have a great deal of house cleaning to attend to."

"Who was fishing on the *Filet & Release* yesterday?" Torgensen asked, getting right to the point.

Devin replied, "We've all used that boat. Some fished from it yesterday and some the day before. Why do you ask?"

The officer continued, "With the number of guests you have here, you have grossly exceeded your limit of halibut, even if all of you were fishing on it at the same time... which, of course, would also be a violation. Give me your licenses immediately!"

All complied, except VanTassle. "I do not believe you 'ave ze jurisdiction over me. I am ze Dutch citizen!"

"Well, that and a dollar might get you a hot cup of coffee over in Hoonah!" Torgensen retorted. "Hand me your license right now or I'll transport you there and placed you in detention. I just might do that, anyway."

The officer studied each license and then continued, "I'm looking closely at these licenses and not one of them indicates permission to hunt and kill sea lions. Does anyone contest that conclusion? I didn't think so. So, why is there one piled in the back of your boat, on top of the halibut?"

The men stared blankly at Torgensen.

"In addition, when I tied up to your dock, I observed another violation of the law. In fact, this one ranks as your biggest violation to date. I found two bald eagles washed up on shore and they were full of buckshot. There's not a license available for that one. Unless someone here is over fifty percent Tlingit and can show me the proper credentials and authorization, all of you are in jeopardy on that count. Does anyone here have an authorization to kill eagles?"

Again, the officer was met with blank stares.

"Well, I didn't think so on that one, either. I'm placing all of you under arrest on three counts. First, for grossly exceeding your halibut limit, second, for killing a sea lion without authorization and third, for violating a most serious federal law: killing two bald eagles. I need not remind you that eagles are protected, and I'll add that they are a very revered bird around these parts.

"Everyone get dressed immediately. We're headed to Hoonah for a visit with the magistrate. Knowing how hard she comes down on wildlife violators, I suggest you bring a heck of a lot of cash along with you. You're going to need it for bail!"

CHAPTER NINETEEN

THE MAGISTRATE

None of the fishermen were at the lodge on Thursday morning, nor were they out on the water fishing. Instead, Devin McMichaels and his guests were inside the Hoonah court room, being introduced to the newly elected magistrate, Susan Tyler. Only the twins were still at the lodge, since they had not been accused of participating in any of the crimes.

Even though the village of Hoonah is designated as an "Unorganized Borough," such a designation does not mean it is a community without a system for law and order. The Hoonah-Angoon region is one of several census districts that has the option of providing justice by way of tribal government.

Since Alaskan statehood in 1959, legislation has often been presented to incorporate this sector into an existing borough. Many residents, however, have been vociferous in arguing their opposition to incorporation as a borough, stating that "the status quo suits them just fine."

It has been rumored that the *Brotherhood*, for their own purposes, was the financial force behind the well orchestrated opposition. It has never been a secret that Hoonah residents like their form of self-governance.

The courtroom gallery was packed. Although a recent census recorded less than nine hundred citizens in the community, half of which were native Tlingit, the court room and surrounding areas were overflowing. Many were in attendance to personally witness the day's proceedings, since the tribunal was the only event of note on that particular Thursday. With limited seating capacity inside the court room, many locals were content to stand in the hallways or find a coveted spot near an open window.

The proceedings at hand were not billed as the "trial of the century." They were not even broadcast from neighbor to neighbor as the "trial of the week." However, there were no cruise ships in port, along with their accompanying entourage of trinket buying tourists, and there were no other out of the ordinary attractions of interest on the picturesque horizon that day. The activity at town hall, therefore, was in fact the only show in town!

Hoonah natives had long since filled their personal quotas of bear sightings. Everyone who cared to do so had already enjoyed ride-after-exhilarating-ride down the cable billed as the "longest zip line in the world." They had all pulled crab cages and fished for world record sized salmon and halibut ad infinitum.

With all that being said, on this particular Thursday, the only entertainment Hoonah had to offer was the spectacle of eight sport fishermen and a lodge keeper standing before Magistrate Sue Tyler, up to their eyeballs in legal trouble.

Conspicuous in the gallery were representatives from the local chapter of the *Brotherhood*, including Ponch Marchbanks, Jared Long, Keith Skaflestad, Snook McGee, John Crabill, Bruce Gordon and several others.

On a moment's notice, a contingent representing the Elfin

Cove Chapter of the same fraternal order were present to assist and support their brethren. Among them were Dan Baxter, Jerry Sheldon and newly initiated members, Yosif Kulavik and Boris Konovalov.

As was often the case, the *Brotherhood* was shown overwhelming support from the townspeople.

The newly elected magistrate was the most recent of a long list of fair minded, female civic officers in Hoonah. She was selected for the position, with duties similar to those of a judge, because of her many years of good judgment in the community. Sue and her husband, Wes, owned and operated the town saw mill and were highly respected citizens.

Magistrate Tyler banged the gavel on her desk and brought about silence in the town hall courtroom.

"The proceedings of this court will come to order," she stated firmly. "Will the arresting authority please step forward and present the accusations against the defendants?"

"Yes, your honor. I'm Andy Torgensen, a wildlife officer for the State of Alaska, and I will present the case before us today.

He continued, "I was contacted early this morning by Mr. Jared Long, who is seated in the courtroom gallery. I was informed by Mr. Long that certain sport fishermen, who were staying at a lodge over at Excursion Inlet, were over harvesting halibut.

"He further told me that physical proof of their egregious and highly illegal violations could still be found in their fishing vessel, the *Filet & Release*, which was tied to their dock.

"To perform my sworn duty to the best of my ability, I immediately went to the Hoonah Harbor, boarded my water craft and proceeded in haste to the *Alaskan Bear Lodge*. To carry out my official responsibilities, I did so even though boating conditions were very questionable, at best."

"What did you discover there?" the Magistrate questioned.

"It was just as Mr. Long indicated. The *Filet & Release*, which I found tied to the dock in front of the lodge, was filled to overflowing with halibut. Shockingly, I also discovered a recently slain sea lion inside the boat, lying on top of the halibut.

"As I proceeded down the pier walkway from the floating dock to the shore, I also identified two deceased bald eagles that had washed ashore. I picked them up for examination and saw that they had died from gunshot wounds. A skeet thrower was set up on the nearby sea wall, so I concluded that those who were shooting skeet were also responsible for shooting these protected birds."

"It could not have been me!" Peter VanTassle shouted from his seat alongside the other accused men. "I took but vun shot at ze clay pigeon when both birds dropped from ze sky!"

"Order!" commanded the Magistrate as she rapped her gavel. "In due time, you will have your turn to rebut. Do not speak out again or I will hold you in contempt. Carry on, Officer Torgensen."

"I then sought access to the lodge tenants, first asking for their licenses. When I had them in hand, I began my questioning. Soon, it was obvious that they were all guilty on all charges. Therefore, I arrested them and brought them across the Icy Strait to your courtroom. I knew you would mete out the justice that this band of lawbreakers deserve."

"Very good, Officer Torgensen. "I'd now like to hear from the defendants. Gentlemen, will you please select an individual from your group to represent you?"

Immediately, Peter stood up and boldly stated, "I am ze man! I have ze Juris Doctor Degree from ze Amsterdam University and am ze only one qualified to represent zis case!"

He stepped forward from his position and approached the bench. "May I have ze word in private vith Your Honor?" he requested.

As he bolted forward, the others in the group began arguing with one another. No one wanted Peter to represent them individually or as a group.

"I sure the hell don't want to end up hanging upside down in chains again," Dusty told the others.

"Don't worry," Ty retorted. "With that European as our lawyer, they won't hang us in chains. They'll just take us outside and shoot us!"

It was too late to stop VanTassle. He was at the Magistrate's bench, standing nose to nose with Her Honor. Seeing the two engaged deeply in dialog, the Wildlife Officer knew he must become part of the exchange. When he started rushing to the bar, he was stopped in mid-step by the rap of the judge's mallet.

"In the process of these arrests," she asked Andy, "did you happen to read the defendants their rights?"

Torgensen was speechless. Finally, he broke the silence by mumbling, "Hmmm. No. I did not, Your Honor. There was a terrible gale blowing through this morning... we had six foot seas... I felt lucky to have survived the trip across the Strait... in the confusion... no. I failed to read them their rights."

"Case dismissed!" The Magistrate swiftly hit her gavel on the corner of her desk. "All that have been accused are free to go. But if you are smart, you won't do anything like this ever again! Now, go get your halibut processed. Get the fish filleted and frozen before they spoil!

"Officer Torgensen, I'm ordering you to get these people back to their lodge immediately.

"This court is dismissed!"

The men of the *Brotherhood* were not a happy consortium. Immediately after the Magistrate's quick (and to them, unjust) dismissal of the case against their sport fishing foes, they called an emergency meeting. Along with the fraternity's visiting members from Elfin Cove, they walked together in a pack from the courthouse building to Grandma Nina's Café. It was only a few blocks away from the court room, but it was far enough for them to reconvene in private. They sought time together for a late lunch and to consider their options.

Grandma Nina's Café

The impatience of the seamen was evident and soon their imposing physical presence took its toll. It took but a few minutes for the small contingent of locals that were hanging out in the dining area to clear the building. The uncomfortable band of Tlingit natives finished eating their halibut tacos and then, one by one, they shambled out of the café and walked northward, where they sensed they were in safer climes.

When the locals left, Keith locked the door behind them. The *Brotherhood* was not to be disturbed.

"We should'a burnt 'em out! I knew it, an' I wuz right!" McGee scowled. "At least, my methods git results!"

"Snook! Will you settle down?" Ponch countered. "What we need is a plan... not a bunch of wild talk about what we should'a done. I'm not happy with the Magistrate's decision, either. She'd better not think she can scuttle the *Brotherhood* with her little loopholes in the law! Otherwise, Hoonah will need a new Magistrate. At the very least, we need to send a strong message to the current one. Someone needs t' put her on notice!"

"I'll take care of it, sir." Snook swore under his breath. "I'll take care of it m'self!"

"What about them damned sport fishers?" Jared interjected. "They still need to pay for their sins! Instead of gittin' the punishment they deserved, they got rewarded with a boat full'a halibut!"

"Yeah," Skaflestad shouted from the kitchen where he was fixing halibut tacos for his friends. "They not only made off with

MY halibut, but that wuz a pretty good-sized sea lion they got, too! I could'a skinned him for the hide!"

"Ok, let's organize this then," the Master commanded. "Snook, go git a good boat fueled 'n ready to go. Long, you 'n Baxter 'n Kulavik... take some of the other men and go git the *Rig* up an' runnin'. I'll get *Sweet Cheeks* and do an air recon. Then I'll let ya' know where them boys are fishin' later today. It's time for *Brotherhood* justice t' be served! This here meetin' is formally ajurn'd."

"Jared," McGee nudged his former first mate. "B'fore ya go t' git the *Rig* ready, grab Baxter and come w' me. We have some overdue Magistrate business t' take care uv.

"Let's go see if'n her ol' man's saw mill is fireproof!"

CHAPTER TWENTY

REDEMPTION

Wes Tyler insisted that his crew of hard working employees shut down the Icy Straits Saw Mill early in the afternoon, hoping everyone could get home to their families in time to enjoy a reasonably good head start on the weekend.

Despite the harsh gales and the pelting rain that had hit earlier that morning, the skies had cleared before noon and there was a very good chance of warm, sunny weather for a few days.

"Both of my boys are in town," Wes confided to Tom Wehnes, a talented woodworking artist and Wes' good friend.

"It's been awhile since we've had both Ryan and Brice here at the same time and Sue and I want to take them out to Fresh Water Bay for an evening picnic. We need time together to get acquainted with Brice's new fiancé."

For many years, Wes had enjoyed success logging in and around Alaska's southeast, but since buying the mill, his hands had been more than full. Escalating fuel prices, along with decreased business because of the downturn in the economy, were taking their toll on the financial stability of the operation. Nevertheless, he maintained his naturally cheerful attitude, even in the face of adversity.

The people of Hoonah had confidence in Wes and Sue, which, in part, was why Sue was recently elected to be the new Magistrate. Both were hard working and the saw mill employees were loyal and appreciated his kindness and generosity. Always a gentleman, Wes Tyler was known throughout the region as a man in whom there was no guile.

"Later on, my wife and I might also go out to Fresh Water Bay for a picnic," Tom replied. "We're due for a little rest and relaxation, also."

After the employees finished putting away their equipment and tools, the mill was closed and they left together in a car pool, driving hurriedly down the winding back road from the mill toward Hoonah. Always last to leave, Wes followed in his forest ranger green Suburban. He drove out of the yard and pulled to the side of the road, just beyond the property gate. There, he put the aging Chevrolet in park, got out and swung the single pipe gate across the entrance, wrapped the chain around the post and secured the padlock that linked the chains. The Icy Straits Lumber Mill was closed for the evening.

"I don't know why I bother to lock this place up every night," he mused. "There's not much that goes on around here that needs this kind of security."

After he returned to his Suburban, he gently eased it back onto the dirt road and headed for home. He was unaware of the three men that sat quietly in the front seat of a beat up, rusted out pickup, watching his movements. They were hidden from sight, high above the saw mill, on a turnoff road that had been cut into the mountainside long ago.

When Wes' Suburban was satisfactorily out of sight, the trio shared what remained of a pint of *Captain Morgan Spiced Rum*.

After the last drop was consumed, the dark Toyota with its disheveled, unwashed passengers lurking inside, slowly crept from its place of obscurity and trailed down the potholed road, winding along toward the saw mill entrance.

Pulling into the thick roadside bushes, twenty yards before reaching the gate, the men exited the truck. One carried a five gallon can of gasoline and the other two were armed with Scripto fire starters.

The only words spoken as the men stealthily found their way toward the large equipment and lumber filled building used by Icy Straits Lumber, was from the most disheveled member of the trio.

"Ok, boys. Let's go 'n see if'n the ol' man's saw mill is fire-proof!"

The Icy Straits Lumber Mill

After the fuel was liberally doused inside one of the saw mill buildings, a rag was torched and thrown. Immediately, McGee, Long and Baxter dashed out of the blazing shadows of the combusting mill and raced to the safety of their pickup. After stumbling over each other to get inside the cab, Snook turned the ignition. However, to add to the trio's increasing panic, the old Toyota failed to start.

Yelling obscenities at one another, they anxiously exited and began pushing the old heap until they reached the top of a rolling decline in the road. By pointing the truck downhill, the old rattletrap quickly built up enough speed to start the engine by popping the clutch. When the motor caught, McGee and his boys high tailed it back to Hoonah as fast as they dared speed down the winding dirt lane.

"Onc't we git back, let's split up, jest t' be safe," suggested Snook. "I'll hitch a ride with Ponch t' git out'a town and th' two of you round up the others an' git to th' *Rig* with Skaflestad in the *Karen-Marie*. We want t' be seen as far away as possible from the mill!"

"Good plan," Jared agreed. ""The *Brotherhood's* been waitin' at Grandma Nina's, so let's get back over there. We can make it look like we were there all along."

"Once we're inside," Snook instructed, "I'll leave with Ponch for Excursion and make sure we're seen in town. You'd best give me an hour head start b'fore the rest of ya' leave Hoonah."

Just as they reached the city limit sign, the men heard a loud boom coming from the direction of the saw mill. They left Front Street by taking the first right hand turn, then went up the road for a block and turned north. From there, they drove carefully until reaching the back side of Grandma Nina's Café.

Jared and Dan slinked around the small building and stealthily entered through the front door while Snook slithered in through the "Employees Only" back door. When he was inside, the Cap'ting snatched Ponch by the arm and pulled him toward the door. When they walked out, he made sure they were seen exiting the café together.

Front Street had filled with curious spectators who were looking and pointing toward the billowing black smoke on the hillside, across Hoonah harbor toward the west.

"Let's git out'a here an' go take the *Solstice* back from those Faro cheatin' thugs," Snook patronized. "Jared and Dan'll round up the others and join us out in the Icy Strait."

Together, they crossed the street and casually sauntered down the walkway to the seaplane dock where Ponch had tethered *Sweet Cheeks*. As they walked to the pier, Snook continued to salt his alibi by going out of his way to greet every passerby and join them in wondering what had caused the loud explosion and billowing smoke over in the direction of the saw mill.

The following day, an article appeared in the *Juneau Empire Newspaper*, chronicling the saw mill fire:

EXPLOSION AND FIRE
DESTROYS HOONAH SAW MILL
By Klas Stolpe

Juneau Empire Newspaper

"It looked like a howitzer shell hit it."

That was how Hoonah police chief John Millan described the scene Thursday after an explosion and fire destroyed the commercial saw mill belonging to Icy Straits Lumber & Milling, Inc. on Long Island near Whitestone Community, the site of a former logging camp that is a 15-minute drive from Hoonah.

"I served in Iraq and that is what it looked like, like a howitzer had ripped that place apart. The building is completely destroyed," Millan said.

The mill, which employs about 10 workers, operated normally Wednesday.

There were no deaths or injuries and no one was believed to be in the building when the explosion occurred, Millan said.

Hoonah police lead dispatcher Joan Howell had just arrived at work when the first explosion occurred...

"I could feel the blast," Howell said. "It was just a huge, massive explosion. I just thought 'What the heck was that.?' I was standing facing Long Island when it went off."

Howell dispatched emergency personnel to the scene as 911 calls began flooding the station.

Millan arrived to the scene 10 minutes later to see a huge black mushroom cloud still filling the air from a second explosion occurring 30 seconds after the initial blast.

Millan said the black smoke was indicative of a petrochemical fuel source. The remaining debris was completely engulfed in flames and stacks of lumber ready for shipment and sale were ablaze. Smaller explosions continued as emergency crews arrived.

Hoonah firefighters and EMS quickly arrived on the scene and battled to contain the fire from spreading to a mountain-sized pile of sawdust down an adjacent embankment.

US Forest Service firefighters arrived within hours to assist and the state Fire Marshall's office had investigators on the scene. However, they have yet to determine the cause of the fire.

"We don't know what it was," Susan Tyler, who co-owns the Icy Straits with husband Wesley, said. "We think that a fire started in the mill and when it got to oil, that was what caused the explosion. The sad part is we were just getting ready to start a yard in Juneau. Our life's savings were in that mill."

Additional fuel explosions remain a threat to the sawmill storage so firefighters are continuing to saturate the area with water. No other hazardous materials are believed to be on site except fuel oil and hydraulic fluid.

The loss of the mill, in operation for seven years, is a serious blow to the town, said Hoonah City Administrator Bob Prunella, since the lumber sales were used for building and construction projects locally and abroad.

"It looked like a war zone," Prunella said. "This is a loss of jobs we just couldn't afford to lose."

■ ■ ■

During the brief plane ride from Hoonah to Excursion, Snook committed Ponch to join him in his private intrigue to get back the ownership of the *Rig*.

When they landed in the water near Russian Hump, the seasoned bush pilot carefully taxied to the *Rig's* aft and held steady as Snook extended the adjustable arm of a light weight gaff. He deftly caught the hook onto the rear anchor rope and gently pulled the seaplane next to the old boat. When close, he lunged toward the vessel and caught the railing. In one motion, he swung himself over the side and crash landed on the rear deck.

Ponch withdrew the gaff from the anchor rope and used it to

push himself away from the *Rig*. He then powered up *Sweet Cheeks* and taxied in a northeast direction, aiming his pontoons toward the distant Ocean Beauty Cannery.

Before gathering sufficient speed, he pulled back the stick, prematurely trying to gain altitude. At the hands of a lesser pilot, the old crate could have blown the oil cap and might have been buried at sea, but Ponch went through the emergency exercise just for the exhilaration. Once again, he laughed at fate and banked to the right with his starboard wing grazing the water as the plane groaned and lifted into the air.

Snook watched in a stupor, knowing he needed Ponch to succeed. Without him, his own plan of redemption was certain to fail. When *Sweet Cheeks* achieved flight, the grizzly sea captain breathed an audible sigh of relief and proceeded to set his scheme in motion.

In earnest, Snook went into the cabin and fired up the engines. Once they were running smoothly, he exerted himself by partially raising both the front and back anchors. Under normal circumstances, he would have raised them to the top; however, this was not a normal circumstance.

The *Rig* headed south toward the Icy Strait by crossing between the west side of Porpoise and the east side of Pleasant Island. When she was in the open water in the middle of the Strait, he cut the engines and allowed her to drift in the current.

Not long after Snook navigated between the islands, Officer Torgensen and his recently acquitted detainees approached Excursion Inlet. His well-equipped, government issued craft passed on the eastern side of the Porpoise chain as it headed on a northerly course between Hoonah and the *Alaskan Bear Lodge*. Neither saw the other, but Snook knew of the officer's whereabouts from his two way communication with Ponch.

After the exonerated guests were on the floating dock at the lodge, Torgensen headed back toward Hoonah. Timing the current perfectly, the path of the wildlife officer and the veteran pirate intersected in the middle of the Strait. Snook stood at the helm of the *Rig*, excitedly waving his arms to make certain Andy saw that he was in distress.

"Please, sir, bring 'er close so we kin talk," Snook invited.

When Andy was close enough, he cut his engine and threw a tether rope to McGee. They pulled the boats together and tied them. Andy then boarded the *Rig*.

"What's going on?" he queried. "This old boat looks like it's been through a hurricane!"

"She wuz prob'ly torn up in last night's gale," Snook concurred. "No doubt, she's bin abandoned at sea."

The officer acquiesced. "That's what it looks like to me, too. Do you intend to apply maritime law regarding vessels abandoned at sea?"

As if he did not already know the statute, Snook asked for clarification and Torgensen obliged.

"Vessels abandoned at sea become the property of whomever salvages them."

"I'm salvaging this one, then," Snook promptly confirmed. "It wuz mine ons't b'fore and now I'm a'reclaimin' 'er... an' I'm doin' it in yer presence. Do I have t' do anything more to make it official?"

"Not that I know of," the officer replied. "I'll have it researched when I get back to Hoonah and I'll let you know."

"Officer, I'd appreciate it if you'd write up somethin' official sayin' you're a witness that the *Rig* was abandoned. Kin ya' do that fer me?"

Torgensen proceeded to pull a small notebook and pen out of his buttoned-down front pocket and wrote the date, time and his description of the course of events, verifying Snook's salvage rights.

Without any bloodshed, ownership of the oversized fishing vessel was officially returned to its former owner. The *Rig* had been redeemed and Snook McGee was again her captain, but he knew he was soon headed for a showdown with Jared Long.

CHAPTER TWENTY-ONE

MARITIME LAW

Before Cap'ting Snook weighed anchor and steered the *Rig* through the islands and into the Icy Strait, she had remained stoically anchored on the Russian Hump from Tuesday evening when Kustaka had torn through her, clearing the decks of all denizens. After surviving the Thursday morning tempest, she had rested calmly in the water, gently bobbing with the waves and slowly turning with the changing current at the mouth of Excursion Inlet. For that period time, she presented no more and no less the image of an aging, abandoned ghost ship.

For Snook, the timing of the Thursday morning storm was fortuitous. Since all of the *Alaskan Bear Lodge* guests and the lodge keeper left the lodge during the storm (with the exception of the two domestic aides), he knew he had successfully moved the ship before anyone had returned. As long as Yvonne and Yvette had not observed the landing and takeoff of *Sweet Cheeks* (or his removal of the boat), he was in the clear. Other than the eagles perched atop the trees, he was confident that there were no witnesses.

The stage was perfectly set for him to argue, if necessary, that the *Rig* was not set free by any other means than by the winds of nature. If necessary, witnesses could easily be produced verifying that the ship had been abandoned at the Russian Hump.

"After abandonment," he rehearsed in his mind, "the gale blew her off her anchors an' she drifted aimlessly into the middle of th' Strait. No one kin argue th' cause 'n effect. It's a clear case uv abandonment an' jist az Officer Torgensen verified, maritime law sez 'finders-keepers.'"

Even though Snook was comfortable that he had covered his bases, he knew he faced an intense and intimidating confrontation with Jared Long. He buoyed himself with the personal confidence that justice had returned to him that which was his all along.

When the *Karen Marie* left Hoonah Harbor, Jared, Dan, Yosif and Boris were on board with Keith. Their objective was clear. They were intent on getting the *Rig* back into operating condition so that, with the aid of the air reconnaissance provided by Ponch, they could track down the whereabouts of the *Solstice*. The Brotherhood was unified behind finding a way to reclaim the commercial fishing boat and return her to her proper owner.

In the recovery process, if a sport fisher or two (or more) became casualties, then, so be it! They presented the solid appearance of a determined and focused troupe of crusaders.

When Skaflestad first sighted the *Rig* floating listlessly in the Icy Strait current, he alerted the others. "Look dead ahead," he thundered. "There's the *Rig*. Looks like she's broken free from her anchor! Look there, directly in front of us!"

All hands were on deck immediately and Jared was visibly shaken with the sighting.

"I put down the anchors myself and that storm wasn't strong enough to pull 'em off the bottom. Something's wrong, here!"

When they pulled alongside the *Rig*, Dan grabbed the limp anchor rope and pulled on it. "It's still down there, but it isn't hooked up. It must've pulled free in the storm last night."

"There were two anchors," Jared reminded him. "One at the bow and one at the stern. Oh well, at least she's safe and sound and didn't run aground on one of the islands."

At the moment he finished his sentence, Snook appeared over the port railing. "She's safe 'n sound all right, boys. Me 'n Ponch saw that she was abandoned and floating at sea, so's we landed and claim'd 'er! The law of the sea sez an abandoned ship can be claimed and kept by them that find 'er. I found 'er an' she's mine agin, legal 'n proper. An' I have a signed statement from an officer-of-th'-law sayin' so."

Jared was furious. With one leap, he grabbed the anchor rope and, hand-over-hand, he climbed to the top of the railing and vaulted over the side of the boat.

In an instant, he had both hands in a strangulation lock, wringing Snook's neck before the victim had a chance to pull away. It was fortunate for Snook that he had been working in the engine room and still held a crescent wrench in his right hand. If he had not been able to pound Jared on the back of the head with the wrench, he soon would have died from suffication.

When Jared's body went limp, his vice-like grip on Snook's neck relaxed and the Cap'ting was able to gasp for air. In under a minute, his purpled skin returned to its ordinary sunburnt and weather hardened appearance.

As the action accelerated, the rest of the crew who were watching from the *Karen Marie* shinnied up the anchor rope. One at a time, they climbed aboard the *Rig*.

Dan arrived first and was in time to catch Jared as he slumped to the floor, unconscious from Snook's blow.

Keith was next and was just in the nick of time to grab Snook's wrist as he attempted to finish Jared off with a crescent wrench blow to his face. Skaflestad's powerful grip stopped Snook's strike in mid-air and he pulled him down onto the deck, where he lay spread-eagle over him until he calmed down.

"I aughta' kill 'im," was the mantra Snook kept repeating. Finally, however, his temper stabilized and he quit resisting Skaflestad's restraints. "I'm over it now," he promised. "You kin let me up. I won't hurt 'im now."

Jared regained consciousness after Konovalov dumped a bucket of ice cold ocean water on his head.

"What...? Let me up! McGee, this is my boat, not yours. You've got no right to steal it away from me!"

Hesitatingly, Jared got to his feet and staggered back and forth before gaining his equilibrium. He held his hand over the bleeding gash on the back of his head and then slumped back onto the deck.

"Give me a minute," he mumbled. "I'll be okay in a minute."

Finally, when they were both calmed down, Snook looked Jared squarely in the eye and spewed, "This is my boat, Jared. I brought it over from Kamchatka in dangerous waters to be used by the *Brotherhood*. Then, I wuz cheated out of it over in Elfin Cove and by fate, it's mine onc't a'gin. I still want you t' be m' first mate. So, let's be ship-mates a'gin and run this ship like we'd done b'fore. What'd ya say?"

Jared knew he was beat. It was Snook's boat and both he and Dan knew it had been won by using gold stolen from Snook's drawer. He knew fate had returned the *Rig* back to Snook and he knew it was right.

"Yeah, I'd like that," he replied. "I'd like to be yer first mate again and run the crew. I'll be loyal and do the job right, just like I did before."

The two men stood up and off squared with one another. Using the inviolable *Brotherhood* handshake for all their fraternal brothers to see, they duly solemnized a return to their old maritime relationship. Cap'ting McGee was relieved to be the recognized captain of his ship once again.

Retaking command of his boat, the Cap'ting organized his crew and they unified to restore the ship to a pristine, sea worthy state.

Skaflestad debarked the *Rig* and re-boarded the *Karen Marie* to head back to Hoonah. Meanwhile, the men remaining on board knew they had their work cut out for them. Plain and simple, the state of the *Rig* was a mess.

In better times, the worn out sea vessel was never free from barnacles or decay, nor was she visually attractive. However, the engine and equipment rooms were kept in good operating condition. Baxter had always taken personal responsibility to insure that everything functioned as it should.

In order to work on his boat in seclusion, Snook trolled in an easterly direction until they were south of Home Shore, where they reached a small island chain named The Sisters. They anchored the *Rig* in a little cove that was sheltered from the sight and intrusion of others.

Once settled, the crew worked non-stop. Baxter buried himself in the engine room, tweaking and turning engine parts. He banged and kicked some parts; he squirted oil on or wiped grease off of other parts. He manually checked off each mysterious task that mechanics perform to magically transform old engine blocks into well-oiled machines. As he progressed, the incomprehensible contraption began to purr like a kitten.

"...and that, Dan Que Baxter, is why you get paid the big bucks!" Long laughingly commented as he passed by.

"Well, I'm still waitin' for my first paycheck," Dan grinned behind a face covered with grease and engine oil. "And when I get it, I'm not sure it'll clear the bank anyway," he chuckled.

"I know what you mean," the first mate injected. "Take your pay in gold dust, dude. That's what I'm gonna do!"

While Baxter worked on the mechanics and the other men

worked on the facility, Snook and Ponch were deeply engaged in telephone dialog; hatching out scenarios and schemes to retake ownership of the *Solstice*.

Working late, the men finally completed their labors. At twilight, they convened in exhaustion in the mess hall and enjoyed a hearty meal while engaging in seaman banter.

When all had eaten to the point of gluttony, Snook required their undivided attention while he reviewed the following day's plan of action. Every detail and contingency was thoroughly rehearsed until there was no uncertainty as to the execution of the objective.

The men were excused and everyone, with the exception of Boris, retired to their sleeping cabins and drifted into the unconsciousness of sleep until the appointed hour early the next morning.

Boris was assigned night watch duty and he grudgingly set up his sentry at the bow of the boat.

That evening, the Northern Lights broadcast their prism-like colors across the Alaskan sky. Their hypnotic beauty and the gentle rocking of the boat, coupled with Boris' long day of labor, soon took its toll. The Russian's baritone, rhythmic snoring added a humorously musical element to the otherwise tranquil night.

CHAPTER TWENTY-TWO

THE GAFF HOOK

When Dr. Nielson bantered that he had not caught enough salmon to get a decent case of salmonella, the management of the *Alaskan Bear Lodge* called Grantley. *Moore Charters* was contracted to return to the lodge to help the guests improve their catch.

Due to the ongoing drama and distractions that had occurred during the week, each guest had only managed to catch half of a box of filleted and frozen salmon. Thanks to the misdeeds of the *Brotherhood*, they had reaped a plentiful harvest of halibut, but their take of salmon was still woefully short.

Since a fifty pound box of frozen salmon fillets per guest had long been the lodge's unpublished minimum, Devin took the standard initiative to insure his lodgers would leave with a full box, which was to call *Moore Charters* into action.

Promptly at 7:00 a.m., Grantley tethered the *Equinox* to the rustic wooden floating dock at the end of the pier in front of the lodge.

As he had witnessed many times in the past, Captain Moore laughingly watched the sleep deprived fishermen stagger out the front door of the lodge, each pausing on the porch to stretch, before slipping into wading boots and pulling on their rain gear. Invariably, they would stumble across the covered deck of the cabin, then hobble down the stairs and meander down the pier walkway until finally reaching his boat.

The first four exiting the lodge were Nielsen, Hulme, Ford and Trail. One by one, they boarded the *Equinox* and sat in the cabin, doing their best to catch a few more minutes of sleep before leaving the dock.

After five minutes more, Liddiard, O'Neal and Jameson found their way to the *Solstice*, which was tethered opposite the *Equinox*. Once there, they helped one another distribute and organize their fishing gear and then passed along the lunch and snack containers that had been prepared the night before.

After the preparations and work had been finished, assuming his timing was good, Peter VanTassle sauntered out of the lodge and crossed the porch deck. He made a point of taking his time while putting on his boots and rain gear. Gingerly, he proceeded to find his way down the stairway and across the boardwalk.

"Glad you could join us," Liddiard said sarcastically. "Now that all the work is done and we're ready to shove off, is there anything else you would like us to do for you, Mr. Juris Doctor?"

"Oh, yes," he teased back. "You can enlighten me as to how two eagles could be shot down vith vun zingle shot?"

"Ha! It can only be that you made a split second geometric calculation, Peter! Now, please get yourself into the boat. We need to go catch some salmon."

The *Equinox* pulled away from the dock and smoothly sped southward toward Home Shore. The *Solstice* followed closely behind with the other four sport fishermen on board. In less than ten minutes, both boats passed Windy Creek and pulled alongside the Log Dump where they slowed to three knots and began putting their lines in the water. This was their last day to fish and they all wanted it to be a successful one.

Grantley was in his element as he taught the novice fishermen the "how's and why's" of fishing for salmon. He expertly assisted each angler as they reeled out their lines and began trolling. He also showed them how to set their lures at different depths and distances from one another.

The lines were in the water only a matter of minutes when the excited shout of "fish on!" was echoed on board and each man scrambled to his respective fishing pole to secure the first and, of course, the biggest catch of the day.

Trolling parallel to them, about one hundred feet away and slightly to the south, they watched as their fishing mates aboard the *Solstice* were also enjoying success. The Coho were running at Home Shore!

As the morning progressed, both boats filled their wells and each fisherman neared their legal limit for Coho. The fish were large, fat and healthy. The fishermen were satisfied with their end of the week fishing success and they felt restful contentment within the beauty and serenity of the "Great Land" surrounding them. Surely, the fishing gods were smiling down as the boats gently trolled along-side each other.

Even the usually disparaging Peter thought it was a wonderful Friday to be on the water, boating and fishing with good friends.

For a perfect day, Grantley intended to give his clientele one last opportunity to catch Kings. He waived over the *Solstice* and instructed Dusty to follow him to Point Couverden.

"It isn't far," he informed the others. "Couverden is just be-yond where the Icy Strait intersects with the Lynn Canal, just north of Rock Island."

Ponch had spent the morning patrolling along the Icy Strait and into Excursion Inlet. He was carefully watching for the whereabouts of the *Solstice*. When he flew over the *Alaskan Bear Lodge*, he knew firsthand that his former catamaran was no longer docked there. He therefore patrolled the waterways patiently, suspecting correctly that she was in use and her passengers were trolling for salmon somewhere in the vicinity.

"Since the best fishing in these parts is within a short distance of the lodge," he reasoned under his breath, "there wouldn't be a reason for them to fish anywhere else." He continued flying *Sweet Cheeks* at an altitude that did not appear suspicious to the fishermen below; nevertheless, his reconnaissance was close enough to the sea to identify the water craft below.

When the *Equinox* and *Solstice* were leaving Home Shore, the crafty bush pilot spotted his prey. He radioed Snook and reported "our quarry is in full sight and is rounding the south end of Home Shore. They appear to be headed toward the Lynn Canal. The *Solstice* is fishing in tandem with the *Equinox*."

"Our planned encounter could not be scripted to take place in a better location," Ponch contemplated. "It's better because the Lynn Canal is a larger and more imposing body of water than the trolling area along Home Shore. More importantly, however, there will be far fewer boats and witnesses in the Lynn Canal than there are at Home Shore."

The Master gave the order for Snook to pull anchor and move from the Sisters toward Lynn Canal. He further instructed to "stay out of sight as much as possible!" He told Snook to cease movement while still out of the field of vision of the *Solstice* and *Equinox* and to drift somewhere along the southwestern side of Rock Island.

. . .

The *Brotherhood* regrouped well beyond the sight of the twin catamarans while the sport fishermen were busy pulling more

Cohos and an occasional Chinook out of the sea. They were gleefully oblivious to the firestorm that was heading their way.

"That's about our limit," Grantley informed his fishermen as Jeremy, while shrieking loudly, reeled in another King salmon. "I'm glad you guys paid extra to get your King stamps since they're running hot today. Let's tie ourselves up to the *Solstice* and count our fish. We might be over our limit for the day."

"Yeah, that and the fact that I'm getting carpal tunnel from reeling so much," Karl admitted with a grimace. "Even if we don't have our limit, I think I'm done!"

"Let's count 'em anyway," protested Shawn. "If we're as much as even one fish short in any species, I'll do the reeling, Doc! We're finally out on the water enjoying world class fishing. If our luck holds and we get more strikes, I'm willing to reel 'til my arm falls off!"

"Let's see how the guys in the other boat have done," Moore repeated. He waived at the *Solstice* and yelled for them to reel in their lines and bring their boat alongside the *Equinox*.

"What's the fish report on the *Solstice*?" he asked Gary.

"We've maxed out on Silvers and Kings," came the reply. "We can keep right on fishin', though," he laughed, "as long as you'll pay the fines!"

"Since you're boat is self-guided, you can catch double what I can on my boat. Being a licensed captain does have its drawbacks! Let's do a fish count and see where we stand."

■ ■ ■

Within minutes after Snook brought the *Rig* to a stop below Rock Island, Faggan Skaflestad pulled alongside in the *Janice K*.

"Ponch told me to meet you here," he yelled upward to the unscrupulous crew peering at him from above. "He said you'd need my boat for a little dirty work."

Before they could engage in conversation, *Sweet Cheeks* landed nearby and taxied to the starboard side of the *Rig*. Kulavik leaned over the rail with an extended gaff hook and used it to snag the tie down rope. Then he pulled the float plane to the ship and tethered them together.

Konovalov extended a hand to help Ponch transition from the plane to the boat.

Faggan tethered his boat to the *Rig's* port side. He then gingerly climbed up the rope ladder and hoisted himself over the railing and landed flat footed onto the deck.

At the order of the Benevolent Master, all hands stood at attention while listening to their leader's instructions.

"Whatever you do," he concluded after giving specific orders to each man, "don't let either of those fishing boats escape our grasp. Now is the time for us to hoist our fraternal flag! Man yer positions. We commence at exactly zero five hundred hours. It's show time! Play yer parts well, men. Play them well!"

There was no mistaking the intent and resolve of the pirates. Their dark countenances belied their resolve to help their leader regain possession of his commercial fishing boat.

• • •

Going against his nature, Captain Moore empathized with the pleadings of his fishing clients.

"Okay, okay! I believe we can troll for a few more salmon," he winked.

Moore's deck hand had already fileted the day's catch and in the process the fish heads and skeletons had been thrown overboard. "Who can tell how many fish we landed, just by counting the fillets?" Jeremy snickered to the others.

To allow the *Equinox* to technically be "self-guided" and thus, be within the letter of the law, he turned the helm of the Equinox over to Randazzle and changed boats, joining the fishermen on the *Solstice*.

"Now you guys can legally catch a few more Kings," he shouted as the two boats disengaged.

When the catamarans had separated from one another by twenty feet, and just as they started to put their fishing lines in the water, Peter shouted loud enough for all to hear, "Look vat is coming at us from ze south?" All eyes turned.

In a concerned voice, Dusty answered slowly, "I'll be damned. It's that old pirate ship we partied on the other night!"

"This can't be good," Tyrone interjected in an intense and uncomfortable voice. "Those are the thugs that convicted us, hung us upside down, then framed us and got us arrested yesterday."

"Hey, T-Bone," Dusty yelled to Ty. "Tell Randazzle to come back over here next to us. I think all of us should get into Grantley's boat and abandon the *Solstice* before someone gets hurt."

"I think you're right, Dusty," Grantley affirmed. "Those guys are bad news. They're gaining on us, though, so first, let's get some distance away from them before we make the transition."

Grantley leapt to the controls of the *Solstice* and put the hammer down. Randazzle, who was driving the *Equinox*, followed suit. The boats created a massive wake as both soon reached their maximum speed and planed out on the water at thirty five knots.

Pulling around the *Rig* and crashing through the water behind them with speed and momentum, the *Janice K* pulled between the two catamarans. Snook, who was at the helm of the *Janice K*, swerved dangerously close to the *Solstice*, causing Grantley to react by peeling away from the pursuing boat. Anger began to show on the face of the otherwise laid back charter boat captain.

"You'd better think twice before trying to ram me again!" he yelled as he shook his fist. Following his warning, Moore changed his tactics and pulled alongside the *Janice K*. He screamed for Ty to "take the wheel and continue steady, alongside the adversary. Stay glued smack up against that sucker!" he shouted over the noise of the engines.

Tyrone gritted his teeth and daringly did as ordered.

Grantley then snatched a nearby gaff hook. He jumped athletically onto the back platform of the *Solstice* and, in a single leap, bounded onto the deck of the *Janice K*.

Watching the action closely, Snook followed suit. Yanking Faggan away from his white knuckle grip on the rail, he pushed him to the controls. He then grabbed two gaff hooks, gripping one in each hand and aggressively met Moore midships.

A swashbuckling sword fight with the sharp pointed gaff hooks ensued between the two men of equal size and strength. As they forced one another up and down, and then back and forth, in the large fishing area of the *Janice K*, neither was capable of gaining an advantage over the other.

Hoping to turn the fight in McGee's favor, Faggan watched for an opportunity. When Moore staggered toward the port side of the boat with McGee seeming to be holding his balance in the middle, the old seaman made his move and swerved sharply to the right.

The swift jerk of the boat caused Captain Moore to stagger even faster and he was doomed to teeter out of control and fall overboard. Just before his feet left the ground, using every ounce of strength he could muster, he fiercely swung his gaff. The five inch hook caught McGee, puncturing him through his upper back. The metal gaff pierced clean through him and came out in a bloody gusher near the front of his left shoulder.

In the frantic moment when Moore uncontrollably fell overboard, to avoid going down alone, he viciously pulled McGee with him into the freezing water of the Lynn Canal. Plunging uncontrollably over the side, the two men disappeared from sight before the *Solstice* or *Equinox* could turn around and get back to the site of submersion.

In a panic, Faggan reversed his direction and, at full steam, headed toward the safety of Hoonah.

When the *Solstice* and *Janice K* had engaged one another in battle, the *Rig* set her sights on cutting off the *Equinox*. With a much larger boat on his heels, Randazzle knew the best chance for survival would be through cunning and small boat maneuvers. Therefore, he decided to double back. In doing so, he was able to fly past the *Rig* before First Mate Long could change directions. Looking behind him as he went crashing through the waves, he saw the *Solstice* had turned around and was following his lead.

Concocting a plan for the long run, VanTassle began collecting every bottle, soda pop can and floatable object he could find rattling around on the *Solstice*. Using the puncture blade on his Leatherman, he poked a hole through the sides of each container. Then he pulled the eighty pound test line out of a halibut reel and started to string the mix-matched assortment of objects together, tying knots about five feet apart to keep them separated from each other.

"What's your plan?" asked Dusty.

"Just du vat I'm doing," he answered, "and you vill soon see."

O'Neal and Jameson grabbed every object in sight and followed VanTassle's example. When there were no objects available to string together with the rest, the line appeared to be about forty five feet in length.

"If your plan is to throw the line out to distract our pursuers, they can simply navigate around it," Dusty said.

"For vunce, you may be right. Hand me ze map," insisted Peter. "Ve need to find ze narrow channel for dis to verk."

"Here's your narrow channel," Ty said as he pointed at the Sisters Islands. "If they'll follow us through there, you'll be taking them through a very narrow body of water."

"Ja! That vil verk. Tell Gary to drive through ze middle of ze islands! But stay right in ze middle of ze channel. Zere are ze reefs on both sides. If we hit ze reef, ze pirates vill overtake us and ve vill be... how do you say? Ve vill be toasted!"

Dusty stepped to the cabin door and relayed VanTassle's message. "Gary, go right through the middle of those islands over there. Stay right in the middle and watch for reefs!"

When they neared the Sisters, the *Equinox* cut to the left and pulled alongside the *Solstice*. Randazzle was at the helm and he slowed down to get instructions. The *Rig* was closing in and there was no time for mistakes.

Dusty pointed as he yelled instructions to Randazzle. "Get ahead of us and go full speed, right through the middle of those islands up ahead. Watch carefully for the reefs on each side of your boat. We're going to lure the pirate ship into following us. If they catch us, you guys go like a bat out of hell toward the lodge and radio for help!"

Gary shouted for Ty to come to the cabin. "Spot for me and watch for the reefs," he instructed. "I'm doing my best to drive this thing, but I need your eyes to keep us off the rocks!"

"Keep the throttle down," Dusty roared from the back of the boat. "They're gaining on us!"

Peter attached a bait bucket to each end of the fishing line. Every object tied to the line in between the buckets was lighter than the buckets themselves, so he felt confident of the results when he put his invention into action. Not able to help himself, he lavishly expressed self-satisfaction that his design was perfect and that it was a brilliant plan to fulfill his objective.

"However, I did not make up the idea. I vunce read about dis tactic in a book," he proudly announced. "Now, tell me ven ve reach ze narrowest place in ze channel. If ze criminals driving ze old boat try to go around my trap, zey vill hit ze reef."

Still speaking to Dusty, he commanded, "you vill take ze port side and I vill take ze starboard side. Ven I give you ze signal, throw ze bucket as far away from ze boat az you can. I vill do ze same on dis side."

"Faster, Gary. They're catching up to us!" Dusty screamed over the roar of the engines.

No sooner than Dusty had hollered for Gary to increase his speed, he heard rifle shots coming from the *Rig*. Immediately, he and Peter hit the deck to keep from getting hit.

The shots got louder as the approaching vessel drew nearer. Now less than one hundred yards separated the two boats and the fishermen knew they were running out of time.

"On ze count of three, throw ze bucket vith everything you can muster! Vun. Tui! THREE!"

Both men stood in a crouched stance on opposite sides of the boat and let their respective bait bucket fly with all their strength. As the buckets hit the water, the line strewn with pop cans, bottles, torn towels and other objects followed and made an ever extending line stretching from one side of the narrow channel to the other. The catamaran's wake carried the bait buckets outward, stretching the line to its limit.

Peter and Dusty remained standing, watching to see if their trap would accomplish the desired result. As the *Rig* plowed into the line, since it had neither enough time to slow down nor enough channel to swerve to the right or to the left, the cans and debris disappeared under the bow. In less than a minute, while still sheltering themselves behind the back of the boat to avoid being hit by the onslaught of incoming bullets, they saw the old pirate ship rapidly slow down and then finally grind to a halt.

"You may salute me now, Mr. O'Neal," Peter stated proudly. "That's quite ze mess I have caused to be wrapped around zat old boat's propeller!"

The *Solstice* slowed to a more comfortable cruising speed and, rejoined by the *Equinox*, both boats continued in the direction of Excursion Inlet and their safe haven at the *Alaskan Bear Lodge*. To the fishermen, the *Rig* grew smaller in the distance. However, the scene remained large enough that they all could see the old ship drifting helplessly into the reef.

The men on both catamarans smiled as they saw the crew of the *Brotherhood*, one at a time, climb down a thick rope that was hastily thrown over the side of the ship. Each slapped one another on the back and jeered when they witnessed their adversaries wading waist deep into the icy water toward the safety of the rugged and rocky shores of Sisters Island.

CHAPTER TWENTY-THREE

BIVOUAC

The *Karen Marie* trolled quietly at three knots, parallel to the tree lined Alaskan shoreline. Three fishing poles were secured in pole holders at the back of the boat. One had its lure set on the down rigger at forty feet, another at fifty five and the third at sixty five. Periodically, the fishing lines were watched by Devin McMichaels while Faggan and Keith Skaflestad observed the shoreline.

Although the trio had already landed their limit of salmon on that peaceful Friday evening, they proceeded to troll while they continued their search.

Instead of concern with their fishing poles, however, all three were focused on looking through their binoculars as they sought for signs of an encampment along the picturesque Point Couverden beach.

"There they be!" Faggan exclaimed in his best pirate brogue, while pointing at a distant pair of contented looking men who were sitting on a log while roasting wieners over an open campfire.

"Yep. Same place as last week," Keith replied. "One of these days, we should put some variety into this "Last Frontier" fishing adventure of ours."

Faggan reached across the cabin console and sounded three short blasts on the fog horn. He then sauntered to the back of the boat to help Devin reel in the lines.

"We need to step it up, guys" Keith stated flatly. "I have a whale watching tour scheduled for later tonight. Me 'n my boys need to get the boat cleaned and ready to go before the outing."

Expertly and gently, Keith glided his fishing vessel to the shore at the softest landing spot on the beach.

"Hurry up, this isn't a Boy Scout overnighter!" Faggan yelled to the campers. "Put out your fire and let's get going. You can eat your hotdogs on the boat."

When the pair of look-alike campers were on board, the twin 250's propelling the *Karen Marie* were pulled into reverse with enough thrust to unbeach the craft. Within a minute, the four native Alaskans and the lodge keeper were back into the open waters of the sea and headed toward home.

They boated south until passing the knoll of noisy sea lions that more often than not inhabited Rock Island. Once they passed the barren island, they turned west into Icy Strait and drove in a beeline along the coast toward Excursion.

"That was our best fencing match yet, little brother," Sam laughed. "But to be fair, it should be my turn to fake-harpoon you next week."

"Correction, since I'm three minutes older than you," replied Grantley, "you're the little brother!. And, in my opinion, I don't think we should tinker with the choreography. Our fight scene came off quite well the way we did it today. That new gaff Ponch got us really shoots out a lot of fake blood!"

"Yeah. It looked like the real thing, all right. But just so you know, I bruised my thigh falling overboard today. At the very least, I want to have a stunt double on some of these physical scenes!"

"No way," Grantley laughed. "You *are* the stunt double, remember 'Snookie?' Get used to it!"

"What whimps," Skaflestad interjected. "You're both a pair of mommy's boys! I'd like to see either one of you attempt to jump over the side of the *Rig* and swim to shore in my Sasquatch suit! That thing weighs a ton when it's wet. And when it's dry, it's hotter than Hades inside there! Neither of you could pull off the Kustaka role. Neither of you cupcakes are man enough!"

"Don't break your arm patting yourself on the back, Keith," Devin laughed. "I'll admit, though, you all played your part pretty well this week."

Skaflestad changed the subject. "My dad and I have some commercial fishing to do out at Deer Harbor, so we won't be at the cast party tomorrow. Here's our old shredded backpack. Grantley was nice enough to give it to me over at Nugget Falls the other day. The eight pouches of gold from the Last Chance Mine are inside."

Faggan continued Keith's directions. "Tell Ponch that there's plenty of the yellow stuff in there to pay the cast members for their work this summer. What we don't need can be given back to Renee and Gary over at the Last Chance Mining Museum to be used later. Tell everyone that staging these performances for the *Alaskan Bear Lodge* is getting more fun every week.

"Yep," Keith agreed. "They're fun because we're getting better at it. It's pretty realistic!

"While you're at it, see that Andy and Sue get special recognition. Their thespian talents have improved and it should be mentioned publicly. Likewise, give my best to Ponch and the boys of the *Brotherhood*. They performed well, as they always do."

"I doubt Wes will forget," Sam injected. "But I'll remind him to call his insurance agent about the fire! He's been moaning that he needs a new milling room and better equipment for a couple of years, so I'm glad we found time and a way to squeeze the saw mill fire into this week's sport fishing drama. Knowing Wes, he'll appreciate our thoughtfulness on his behalf."

When the *Karen Marie* passed the *Salmon Run*, Devin instructed Keith to "pull ashore and drop me off at the pier at *Doc Warner's*. I'll hike to my lodge the back way, through the woods. My guests'll be packing and getting ready to go home in the morning and I surely don't want them to see me getting out of your boat. It'll spoil the illusion. I'll bet they're pretty excited to get back home so they can share some of these implausible adventures with their family and friends.

"After all, that's what our *Alaskan Bear Lodge* experience is all about!"

EPILOG

O n schedule Saturday morning, Ward Air's floatplane
landed near the beach in front of the *Alaskan Bear Lodge*
and taxied across the calm, mirror-like water to the
shoreline. Twenty feet from shore, pilot Randy Kiesel pushed hard
on the thrust, causing the aircraft to rotate to the right and coast
backward onto dry ground.

Randy's brother, Ed, cracked open the door on the starboard
side of the plane and yelled over the roar of the engines, "Hey,
Dev! Grab the tail and swing the plane into position."

Eight lodge guests and two beautiful domestic aides posed on
the floating dock while the lodge keeper snapped group photos
for everyone. Afterward, the group formed a fire line and passed
their luggage, one to the other, until every box and duffle bag
reached the plane. The two pilots stacked the luggage snugly
inside the plane's stowage area. As they boarded, each fisherman
momentarily hesitated and looked back before boarding the
seaplane.

Gary Liddiard went back to fishing on the Provo River. It was
rumored that witnesses saw him casting his fly hooks in the
direction of hooligans rafting down the rapids. A *Provo Herald*
newspaper reporter wrote an article detailing that he was cited by
the DWR for "accidentally 'snagging' multiple inner tubes in less

than a half hour span of time. After paying the fine," the article further chronicled, "Liddiard smiled broadly as he lit a Tiparillo and said 'It was worth every penny!'"

Dr. Franklin "Randazzle" Hulme, DDS, returned to the sweltering heat of the Phoenix Valley and was met with a very cool reception by his wife, Gloria. "I can't safely let you out of my sight, can I?" she posed as she looked out the kitchen window, glancing fondly at her twenty something Latino gardener. "Next year, I might go to Alaska with you... but don't count on it," she added with a half-smile as the yard boy smiled back and winked at her. "Don't count on it!"

Jeremy Trail and Shawn Ford opened a branch office in Denver for their insurance agency, where they went to work organizing a comprehensive risk management plan for their new client, Peter VanTassle. They convinced the wealthy magnate to change the name of his trucking company, known for years as "Bovine Transport," to "The Bull Shipper." VanTassle was not sure why they suggested the new moniker, but trusting their judgment, he went with their recommendation. They promised that his risk management documents would be ready for review the day he returned from an anonymously pre-paid *"How to Win Friends and Influence People"* seminar. Reportedly, an unnamed donor had signed him up and paid the fee for the two week course.

Dr. Karl Nielsen returned to his home in the Wasatch Mountains where he retired from his long and successful career in neurosurgery. In addition to devoting his sunset years to hunting and traveling, he aspired to become a paperback writer. Under a pseudonym, his first book was titled *"How I Helped a European Pain in the Posterior Become a Socially Acceptable Human Being."* Therefore, his recent check to The Dale Carnegie Foundation was tax deductible.

Dusty O'Neal and Tyrone "T-Bone" Jameson returned to Hollywood and began collaboration with a screen writer for their new movie, appropriately titled *The Icy Strait*. Both actors anticipated the new film would be a box office smash and purportedly, would feature the debut of two newly discovered bombshells, Yvonne and Yvette Svendsen.

Devin McMichaels busied himself at his lodge by organizing the script for his next group of guests. He then went to Hoonah and joined the cast of characters employed by the *Brotherhood*. The acting fraternity convened each Saturday afternoon at the Hoonah City Hall for fun and fellowship at their weekly cast party.

After dining on fresh crab hors d'oeuvres, washed down with properly aged *Chardonneal*, the troupe divided up the gold nuggets from the Last Chance Mine as pay for their summer performances.

When the festivities subsided, they earnestly studied McMichaels' new script. Well into the evening, those committed to doing "whatever it takes," rehearsed and choreographed the new adventures and daring escapades planned for the next batch of unsuspecting sport fishing guests scheduled to arrive at the *Alaskan Bear Lodge*.

Excursion Inlet, Alaska